The Finding

Nina Bawden

THE FINDING

A Yearling Book

Published by
Dell Publishing
a division of
The Bantam Doubleday Dell Publishing
1 Dag Hammarskjold Plaza
New York, New York 10017

Yearling ® TM 913705, Dell Publishing a division of
The Bantam Doubleday Dell Publishing Group, Inc.

ISBN: 0-440-40004-X

Reprinted by arrangement with William Morrow and Company, Inc., on behalf of Lothrop, Lee and Shepard.

Printed in the United States of America

June 1988

10 9 8 7 6 5 4 3 2 1

CW

To Jo Guthrie
in memory of Niki

Chapter One

No one knew where Alex came from. Only where he was Found.

On the day of his Finding, the mist lay on the river; a soft white blanket on the brown Thames, lazily stirred by the slow tide of the water into smoky tendrils and curls. There was no wind that March Sunday morning, and for a few seconds, just before six o'clock, no sound from the City—no traffic, no horns, no sirens, no bells. Even the seagulls were silent; sleepy and chilled in the dawn. Either side of Cleopatra's Needle on the Embankment, the two huge Sphinxes lay, lion arms outstretched on the parapet, bronze guardians of an Egyptian obelisk of stone.

The left-hand Sphinx, this particular morning, was guarding something else too. In its arms, when Big Ben struck the hour, a bundle began to struggle and cry. A small fist struck out, hit unfamiliar cold stone, and the cries became loud with outrage, startling a gull roosting on the head of the Sphinx. The gull peered down with one yellow eye and flew off down river, mewing a warning.

* * *

Most people know when and where they were born. "A fine boy," the doctor has said. Or, "A beautiful daughter." Later, their father and mother will say, "You were such a funny little scrap, all red and bawling."

"A Finding is more exciting than a Birth," Alex's mother told him. "A Finding is something you should be proud of, something to remember that makes you quite different. Special. Extraordinary."

Alex believed this. "I was Found," he said to his teacher when he first went to school. "I was Found in the arms of the Sphinx in the City of London."

For a while, before he was old enough to know better, Alex thought that the Sphinx must be his real mother. When he was five years old he was taken to look at it, and he touched the stone arm and said, "Hallo, Mum." His parents, his adopted mother and father, looked at each other and smiled, but his sister Laura, who was two years older than he was, turned scarlet with anger. She said, "Don't be stupid, Alex. It's only a statue." And, to the smiling grown-ups looking down at them, "You're stupid, too. It's not fair to tell him such stupid stories."

"Tell me again," Alex said at bedtime that day when Laura was still being bathed by their mother, and their father was tucking him up, saying goodnight. "Tell me about my Finding."

Part of the story his father told was made up to amuse him: how he had cried in the arms of the

Sphinx for more than an hour, frightening the birds that perched on its head and attracting the attention of an old tramp who had stopped and peered and shuffled off quickly. Then (this part was true) a taxi driver on his way home after working a night shift saw the agitated flutter of a pale shawl, a baby where no baby should have been, and got out of his cab to investigate.

From then on Alex's history is known and well documented, written down in police and social service reports and in the files of newspapers. The taxi driver, who had seven children of his own, picked up the cold, angry baby and drove to the nearest police station, where a bottle of warm milk was produced and a doctor called. Then (just as at a Birth) the baby was pronounced well and healthy, about five months old, a fine boy with a couple of teeth breaking pinkly through his sore gums, and a furious appetite. He was wearing a knitted suit, a very wet diaper, and a woolen shawl that was rather old and matted as if it had belonged to someone else or had been carelessly washed in a machine at too hot a temperature. There was nothing valuable on his small person as there would have been in a made-up story: no gold rings or lockets with photographs in them, no embroidered monograms on his garments, no little note fastened to the matted shawl saying *Please care for this baby, his name is Nathaniel*, or *Demetrio*, or even plain *John*. Nothing at all to give what is called "a lead." Someone had left him there, placed him in the arms of a bronze copy of a mythical creature from ancient Egypt, and vanished forever.

For a little while he was famous. His photograph was in all the papers. He was filmed for television, peacefully sleeping on one occasion and bawling on another, in the arms of a pretty nurse from St. Bartholomew's Hospital. The police hoped that someone would come forward to claim him, but although the newspaper stories and the television news programs produced hundreds of letters from people who offered to care for him, none of them were from his real mother or father. In the end Laura's mother and father adopted him as their own little boy. And so Alex lived with them until the real beginning of this story, which is six years after Laura had told her parents not to be stupid on the Thames Embankment in London, and eleven years after he had been found there.

It begins, to be exact, with his grandmother saying, "It's a pity we don't know his real birthday."

She said this in a low voice, muttering to herself, while Alex was blowing out the candles on his cake. He had twenty children to his party and they were all making a lot of noise. Loudest of all were his younger brother and sister, Bob and Ellie, who were standing on their chairs and shrieking, but Alex heard his grandmother in spite of it. He blew out his candles in one hefty puff and went to stand by her chair. He said, "I don't have a birthday. I was *found.* This is my Finding Day."

He thought that perhaps his grandmother had not

understood how important this was, how different it made him. It was something he had been taught to be proud of, and he thought she would be proud as well, once she knew. She said, "Of course, Alex darling, don't pay me any attention. I'm a silly old woman," and she laughed as if this were a joke. But he knew by the way she looked nervously at his mother, her daughter, that he wasn't supposed to have heard what she said and that she was afraid she would get into trouble.

And of course his mother had heard her. She said, "You're right, Ma, that was *frightfully* silly!" She laughed, as if this wasn't a rude thing to say to *her* mother, and went on in a loud, cheerful voice, "Alex has blown out his candles. Come on, everyone, *Happy Birthday to you, Happy Birthday to you, Happy Birthday, dear Alexander, Happy Birthday to you.*"

They all sang, and while they were singing, Alex whispered in his grandmother's ear, "It ought to be Happy Finding, but Mum says most people wouldn't understand that, so we have to let them sing Happy Birthday." He was surprised to see tears in his grandmother's eyes. He said, still whispering, "Don't worry, I won't let her be cross with you," and was more surprised still when she put her arms around him and hugged him and whispered back, "I only said it because you are the dearest little boy in the world, and I wanted things to be perfect."

Luckily, Alex's mother didn't hear that. She was too busy cutting the cake and making sure every piece was exactly the same size. Alex knew she would have been angry if she had heard it because she had been working so hard all day preparing the party, icing the cake, making special rolled-up sandwiches like little wheels—and the pastry balls with spicy cheese inside that was Alex's favorite food at the moment. And she and Dad had given Alex the presents he wanted most: a pair of roller boots and a solar calculator. In fact, the only thing that had made his Finding Day not quite perfect had been the check for twenty pounds that his grandmother had sent him tucked inside his birthday card. Laura had said, "I only got ten pounds on *my* birthday," and their mother had pursed her lips and frowned at their father across the breakfast table.

He had said, "She means well, love. Don't let it upset you."

"She shouldn't give him more than the others. She shouldn't make a difference between them."

"It could be the other way," Alex's father had said. "That would make it worse, wouldn't it?" He had put his hand over hers, squeezing it, and smiled at Alex. "Put it in your Post Office savings book, lucky fellow. It'll go a long way toward your new bicycle."

After breakfast, walking to school, Laura had said, "Gran makes an extra fuss of you because you're adopted. She thinks, poor little fellow."

"That's silly."

"I know. But it annoys Mum. It's as if Gran was saying, you don't look after him properly so I'm making up for it. That's worse than just not being fair to the rest of us. Gran doesn't like Mum sometimes. She looks for ways to upset her."

"But she must like her. Mum's her own *daughter!*"

"You don't have to like your children once they're grown up. Mum bosses Gran about, you know how she does, and Gran likes to get her own back."

Alex sighed. Laura was always making things complicated. He said, rather crossly, "I'm sorry."

"Oh, it isn't your fault," Laura said, being kind now that she saw she had worried him. "If it wasn't you, they'd find something else to quarrel about."

"I'll share the money with you," Alex said. "We needn't tell Gran, but Mum would be pleased and so everyone would be happy."

"That wouldn't help," Laura said. "Just get me into trouble. Putting ideas in your head, Mum would say. Alex, you're such a *dummy*. Don't look so miserable."

"It's you *made* me miserable."

"That won't hurt," Laura said. "Everyone else makes a fuss of you. Someone has to tell you things or you'd never learn anything."

He blinked—no real tears, just a damp gleam in his eyes, and Laura felt both sorry and pleased. Alex was the person she loved best in the world, and she enjoyed making him sad because then she could comfort him. She said, "Come on, cheer up. Let's *run*. I don't mind if you race me. . . ."

He had cheered up then and been cheerful all day, until after the Finding Day party was over. His mother was clearing up and his grandmother was trying to help, putting things in the wrong place as she always did and getting in his mother's way. "Oh Ma, do sit down. I can manage," his mother said, looking suddenly wild-eyed and frantic.

Gran looked at her and put the plate she was carrying down on the table. She hunched her shoulders, shuffled to a chair, and sat down with a groan. "Useless old woman," she grumbled. "Why don't you say it? I thought when I moved to London I'd be a help, not a burden. I'll just sit for a bit and get my breath back, then I'll be off, out of your way."

"You're not a burden, Ma," Alex's mother said. "That's not true and you know it."

"Seems like the truth to me. You never much cared for plain speaking, did you? Always one for pretense and play-acting. You get to my age, you'll find there's no time for that. I'm nothing but an extra load on your shoulders."

Alex's mother said nothing. She piled dishes on a tray and carried it out to the kitchen. Gran leaned back in her chair and closed her eyes. Laura and Alex looked at each other. Laura sucked in her cheeks and pulled down the skin under her eyes to show the red rims, acting old to make Alex laugh. He spluttered, hand over his mouth. He couldn't help it. His grandmother said, "Don't pull faces at me, Laura, d'you think I don't know what you're up to?"

Both children exploded with laughter. Their mother came back with the empty tray. She said, "Laura, will you get Bob and Ellie out of the bath and make sure they have clean pajamas?"

[8]

"Why *me*? Why not Alex?"

"It's his Finding Day. He needn't do jobs on his Finding Day."

Gran snorted. She said something under her breath. Only Alex, who was close to her, heard it. *"Silly nonsense."*

"What's that?" his mother asked.

"Nothing, dear," his grandmother said innocently. "I was just wondering, if you have nothing special for Alex to do, if he'd walk back across the Fields with me. Mrs. Angel was hoping to see him." She smiled sweetly at Alex. "She might have a present, my darling."

Alex said, "Dad will be home soon. He was sorry because he couldn't get back in time for my party, so I thought I'd go to the bus stop to meet him."

It was the nearest he could get to saying that he didn't want to see Mrs. Angel without upsetting his grandmother. He knew that if he looked at his mother for help she would come to his rescue, but that would upset his grandmother more. There was enough trouble between them already, rumbling in the room like underground thunder. So he looked at the floor and his mother said briskly, "Of course Alex will go with you, Ma. He'll have plenty of time with his dad later on." And, as her mother got up from her chair, she put her arms around her and kissed her.

It was growing dark as they crossed Finsbury Fields, the windows in the houses around blooming yellow like the daffodils under the tall bare plane trees. It was the time that Alex liked best; the dusky light made the Fields quiet and secret—a green, secret place in the middle of London. He looked back at his own house on the edge of the Upper Field, and then ahead to the terrace where his grandmother lived next door to her friend, Mrs. Angel. He said, "Look at the lights, Gran; you can see the people inside the houses and they can't see us, like at the theater."

But she wasn't listening. She said, "You're not frightened of poor Angel, are you? When I was a little girl I used to be frightened of very old people. Though she's not so old, really." She sighed and shook her head sadly. "It's sorrow and illness that's aged her."

"I'm not frightened," Alex said. This wasn't quite true. He wasn't afraid of Mrs. Angel in the way he would have been afraid of a wild bull or a savage dog chasing him, but she made his skin creep. *A witch*, he thought sometimes, though he was too old to believe in witches.

"That's a good thing," his grandmother said. "Poor soul. She can't get out, and no one much comes to see her except that dreadful nephew of hers. And he only comes for one thing, as I tell her."

"What's that?" Alex asked. "What one thing does he come for?"

His grandmother didn't answer. She held Alex's hand as they walked up the steps of Mrs. Angel's house, held it extra firmly as she rang the bell. When Alex heard the scrape of Mrs. Angel's walking frame in the hall, he stepped back; he couldn't help it. His

[10]

grandmother squeezed his hand tighter and said, very low, "Just ten minutes, darling. It means so much to her." And then, when the door slowly opened, speaking loudly and brightly, "Here we are, Angel dear. See what I've brought you," as if Alex were a bunch of flowers or a present.

She pushed him in front of her. He kept his eyes on the ground, saw Mrs. Angel's pink-slippered feet, the frilly edge of her nightgown. "Ah, the boy," her voice said, and he looked up reluctantly at the shaky, veined hands on the walking frame, the pink shawl tied across the flat chest, the paper-white face, the black eyes, the almost bald skull—the same pink as the shawl and the slippers—with just a few strands of pale hair hanging down, tangled and soft as a baby's.

To Alex she seemed unbelievably old. But it wasn't her age that made him want to run, nor the sour, kippery smell of the room that she never left now except to shuffle on her walker down the hall to the cloakroom, or to answer the door. He didn't mind when she kissed him, even though the hairs on her upper lip prickled and her mouth was wet. What he hated and had come to dread more and more each time his grandmother took him to see her, which had been about twice a week lately, was the way that she looked at him, black eyes shining like small lumps of coal. It was a greedy look, as if she were hungry. Today, as she settled herself in her chair, silk cushions around her, silk stool at her feet, she actually said the thing that he felt and that scared him. She said,

"Oh, you lovely boy. I could eat you," and as her hands gripped his arms, holding him with surprising strength as they drew him close to her, he felt his stomach turn over.

But all she did was kiss him and squeeze him a little. She said, "Sit down, boy, here on the stool."

He sat where she told him, next to her little feet, feeling the warmth of her leg against him, and looked at the brass clock on the mantelpiece above the gas fire. Ten minutes, Gran had said. Only about eight minutes left now. He sat stiffly, waiting for Mrs. Angel to stroke his hair as she usually did: to let her do that, and to sit still and be quiet while she talked to his grandmother was all she seemed to want from him. She rarely spoke to him directly after she'd kissed him, except once before he left when she said, "Thank you, dear boy, for coming to see me." He thought, his eyes on the clock, on the brass pendulum swinging under the pretty glass dome, *Seven minutes now. That's not long.*

He had almost forgotten that today was a special day. He listened to Mrs. Angel and his grandmother talking, saying the same things that they always said, about Mrs. Angel's nephew and his wife, what they had said last time they had come to see her, how he had been "sharp" and she had been "barely civil."

"Oh, it's always the same when you're old," his grandmother said. "All they want is to stick you away in a home where you'll be no more trouble. Out of the way where they can forget all about you."

That wasn't fair, Alex thought. His grandmother

shouldn't talk like that, as if his mother and father had wanted to get rid of *her* when they'd done just the opposite, persuading her to move from her house in the country where she had been lonely after his grandfather died, and buy a house on the Fields where they could see her every day and look after her.

Then his grandmother said, "I've been lucky. I've got a good daughter. Mind you, things aren't perfect, but we won't say too much about that; little pitchers have big ears, as we know." And suddenly, in a quite different voice, loud and clear as if she were making a public announcement, she said, "It's dear Alex's birthday, that is, what we *call* his birthday, poor little fellow. I did tell you, Angel dear, didn't I?"

"Twice yesterday," Mrs. Angel said. "You told me twice yesterday and again this morning." Her voice sounded irritated though a bit amused, too, the two sounds belonging together like notes in a tune. She touched Alex's hair for the first time since he had sat down on the stool and said, "It's in the drawer in that table beside you."

Alex's grandmother opened the drawer. "Shall I show him?" she said, smiling at Mrs. Angel—an odd, private smile as if whatever there was in the drawer was an interesting secret—and passed a flat oblong parcel to Alex. It was wrapped in brown paper and fastened with ribbon. A book, he thought, as he tugged at the bow. But it wasn't a book. It was a photograph in a silver frame of a girl in a nurse's uniform—an unsmiling face above a white collar, and dark unsmiling eyes looking straight at the camera. Looking at Alex.

"Do you like it?" Mrs. Angel asked. "If you like it, boy, you can keep it."

Alex didn't know how to answer. He disliked being called "boy." He didn't want a photograph of a strange girl as a present.

His grandmother was watching him. She was sitting with her knees apart and her hands on her knees, leaning forward. She was looking excited. A bit like Laura, he thought, when she was about to do something naughty. Though that was silly. His grandmother was too old to be naughty.

She said—burst out with it, as if it were something she couldn't hold in any longer—"It's like him, isn't it, Angel? The mouth, and the eyes. So big and dark, you could drown in them!"

Mrs. Angel took hold of Alex's chin and turned him to face her. She smiled and said, "If you say so, dear." And to Alex's surprise she winked at him. At least, he thought she did; it might have been her eye twitching.

His grandmother said, a bit huffily, "Well, I think it's quite remarkable. Say thank you, Alex dear, for the picture."

"I don't know . . ." he began, and then saw her frowning and jerking her head at him, trying to tell him that whatever he felt he must do as she said. He said politely, "Thank you, Mrs. Angel. It's very kind of you."

[14]

His grandmother said, "It's a picture of Mrs. Angel's daughter, dear. One of her most precious possessions."

He wondered why she wanted to give it to him in that case. There were a lot of pretty things in the room: little china ornaments, a collection of ivory paper knives on a small table, and some beautiful paperweights. He would rather have had any one of these things than an old photograph. He looked at the clock. The ten minutes was over. In fact, almost fifteen minutes had passed. Dad would be home by now. Gran had *promised* him . . .

Mrs. Angel said, "That's all right, Amy. Don't keep on at the boy."

Her voice sounded odd. He looked and saw that her small chin was trembling. His grandmother said, "Wait outside, Alex darling."

He got out of the room as fast as he could and closed the door after him. Through it he could hear Mrs. Angel's soft sobbing, which rose every few seconds to a little hoot like an owl's cry, and his grandmother's voice murmuring kindly.

He opened the front door and looked out. He could see the lit windows of his own house on the other side of the Fields; his mother was in the living room, moving about, still putting things straight after the party. He saw Bob and Ellie, passing the landing window on their way up to bed, his father behind them. Dad paused at the window and peered out, face close to the glass. *Looking for me*, Alex thought, pleased. He stood on the step and waved, but too late. His father had turned away from the window.

Someone had seen him, though. A man, standing under the trees opposite Mrs. Angel's house, moved out of their shadow and crossed the road. He stood at the bottom of the steps and looked up at Alex. He was a tallish man, wearing a brown cap and a raincoat. The light from a street lamp made his eyes look hollow and dark and blackened his mouth, but the raised scar that ran from his upper lips across his right cheek showed up, white and gleaming. He said, "What are you doing here, sonny?"

"Waiting for my Gran."

"Funny place to wait for your Gran. Not her house, is it?"

"She lives next door," Alex said. "She's just visiting."

He stood square in the doorway. Perhaps the man was a burglar. Burglars often lurked on the Fields at night, his grandmother said, watching the houses, waiting until they were empty. The man came closer and smiled, and Alex could see that his upper lip was puckered up, almost split: a harelip. Perhaps he'd been born like that. Unless he'd been in a knife fight.

The man looked uglier when he smiled; the gap in his lip showing stubby brown teeth. "I know your Gran, then. Who she is anyway. What's she up to now? Upsetting my Auntie, I'll bet."

So this was the nephew who was "only after one thing." Alex said, "My grandmother's her friend. She doesn't upset her." He felt doubtful suddenly. Why had Mrs. Angel been crying? He said, "Gran takes me to cheer her up sometimes. She wanted to see me today because it's my birthday."

"Many happy returns," the man said, sounding quite friendly. "Did she give you a present?"

"Well, sort of . . ."

"Care to show me?" The man came up the steps, hand outstretched. Alex unwrapped the parcel and showed him the picture. He felt shy and somehow ashamed, though he had done nothing wrong. He said, "I don't know why Mrs. Angel gave it to me, really. I think it's her daughter."

"That's right," the man said. "Poor old Auntie! Funny sort of birthday gift for you, isn't it? Still, the frame's worth a few bob."

The door of Mrs. Angel's house opened and Alex's grandmother came out and closed it behind her. She said, "Oh!" on a quick, indrawn breath, and then, "Mr. Fowles, isn't it? I don't think we've met. I'm Amy Ross from next door." She held out her hand but the man didn't take it. She said, smiling tightly, "Your aunt's been expecting you. Several days since you've been to see her, I gather. I do what I can, pop in with the odd meal occasionally, but I'm an old woman . . ."

"And a meddlesome one." Mr. Fowles spoke in a calm, even tone.

"I'm sure I don't know what you mean."

"Well, if you don't, I don't know who does."

Alex's grandmother looked at Mr. Fowles levelly, though Alex thought her color had risen. She took Alex's hand and said, "Come on, darling, time you were going home."

As they went down the steps, Mr. Fowles shouted after them, "What are you up to, that's what I'd like to know, you old cow," and his voice wasn't calm any longer; there was an edge to it that made Alex shiver.

But his grandmother only laughed. When Mr. Fowles had gone into the house, she said, "Dreadful man."

"He's horrible. That was a horrible thing to say to you."

"Oh, my shoulders are broad," his grandmother said. "Have to be, at my age, in my situation. Off you go now. Got the picture safe, have you? Would you like me to look after it? In the circumstances, that might be better."

He shook his head. It had been given to him, after all, as a present. It seemed mean not to keep it.

"Suit yourself. But I shouldn't show it to your mother, if I were you. Tuck it under your jacket for now, then put it away in a drawer."

He wondered why she was being mysterious, but then he thought this was nothing new; she often made secrets between them as if she were another child, no older than he was. He was bored with this secret suddenly. He said, "Goodnight, Gran," and ran across the dark Fields, seeing his well-lit home in front of him, the front door standing open, and his father there, looking out. He shouted, "Here I am, Dad," and his father opened his arms for him to run into them. But at the last moment Alex remembered the photograph, the hard, oblong shape under his jacket. He said, "Sorry, Dad, in a hurry; got to go to the bathroom."

He went upstairs to his room, put the picture under his football things in his bottom drawer, went to the bathroom, and flushed the cistern. On his way downstairs he paused for a minute as his dad had done earlier, and looked across the Fields. He could see his grandmother in her house, in her sitting room, and Mrs. Angel in hers. She was standing up, leaning on her walking frame. Then Mr. Fowles, still wearing his raincoat, cut her off from his vision. He walked toward the window and drew the curtains across it.

Chapter Two

It was Laura who noticed that Mrs. Angel's curtains were still closed the next afternoon. Usually the old woman sat at her window during the day, and usually, as she passed her house on her way home from school, Laura waved to her. Laura had never been taken to see Mrs. Angel; she thought that if she waved and smiled Mrs. Angel might say to her grandmother, "Why do you never bring Alex's sister to see me? She looks such a sweet, pretty child."

This particular day Laura was slow going home, taking the long way across the Lower Field where the fair people were churning up the grass with their trucks and caravans, setting up sideshows, round-abouts, flying chairs, and roller coasters for the Easter fair. When Laura had been younger she had thought the fair people were very exciting. Most of them were gypsies who (so her grandmother had told her) some-times stole pretty children, and although Laura knew she wasn't as pretty as Alex—not "striking," which was what people said, meaning that his very dark eyes and flossy, blond hair was an odd combination—she was pretty enough in an ordinary sort of way, blue-eyed, pink-cheeked, and healthy. If the gypsies were to steal her, Laura had thought, her parents would be sorry they hadn't loved her as much as they seemed to love Alex. Now that she was older she had decided that even if it might be a good idea to frighten her mother and father, it would probably not be much fun for her. The caravans looked cramped and uncomfortable, the dogs tethered beneath them bone thin and snarling, and the children who played around the camp were often wailing and dirty. And a fair was not like a circus; running a coconut shy not as interesting as being a high wire artiste or a lion tamer.

She saw that a big tent had been put up on the Upper Field. She wondered if there were going to be a circus this Easter as well as a fair, but when she went to inspect it she found that the tent was arranged like a church. There was a platform at one end, draped like an altar. The people inside, putting out rows of canvas chairs, were very respectable looking: the men in dark suits, the women in smart, brightly colored dresses and hats. A tall, handsome black man smiled down at her. He said, "Good afternoon, sister. Would you like to come to the Meeting this evening?"

Laura smiled back at him shyly. He said, "All are welcome. I am sure that you love the Lord Jesus."

Laura wasn't sure how to answer this. So she said, "How much does it cost?"

"Entry is free," the man said. "All the Lord wants is

your love and your praise. There will be a collection for less fortunate brothers and sisters after the Meeting, but only those whose hearts have been moved will be asked to contribute. It is not money but souls we are seeking."

His kindly eyes shone at her. Laura said, "I don't know. I'll have to ask my mother and father."

"Bring them with you," the man said. "Bring your whole family."

"I could ask my grandmother," Laura said. "She goes to church sometimes."

"May the Lord guide her," the man said. He gave her a pamphlet from a pile on the table at the entrance to the tent.

"Thank you very much," Laura said. He was still beaming benevolently and his shining gaze made it hard to leave. She said, "I'll show my Gran. I'm sure she'll be interested," and backed away slowly. He continued to watch her; when she turned her back she felt his eyes on her still. She had an uncomfortable feeling that if she didn't do what she had said she would, and just went straight home, he would know she had lied and despise her. Her house was quite close; the front door was open and Bob and Ellie were in the little front garden, crouched down on the path, their eyes fixed on the ground. Racing snails was their favorite game at the moment. No sign of Alex, which was a pity because she could have shown him the pamphlet, but it was the day for his judo class. She turned back to the man and said, "My grandmother lives on the other side of the Fields. I'm going there now," and set off at a run.

Going up the steps to Gran's house she saw that Mrs. Angel's curtains were drawn. She didn't think much about it, just registered the fact as she rang the bell and then forgot all about it, because her grandmother opened the door in her dressing gown. Laura had never seen her other than properly and neatly dressed, wearing a pretty frock or a suit with a frilly blouse, and shoes with heels that were much too high (so Laura's mother said) for an old woman. Even though the gown was a smart one, made of blue wool with a velvet collar and cuffs, it was still surprising. "Have you been having a bath?" Laura said. "I'm sorry, I didn't mean to disturb you. I just wondered if you wanted to go to the Meeting."

Her grandmother took the pamphlet and peered at it, holding it close and screwing her eyes up. "No good. I can't read it without my glasses; come on in, Laura my chick. I don't want to get chilled to make matters worse. Your mother will be angry enough as it is."

Following her indoors, Laura saw the sofa drawn close to the fire and a rug lying across it as if her grandmother had been taking a nap. She said, "Why should Mum be angry?"

"She's no right to be," her grandmother said. "I can't help it, but she'll think of a way to make it my fault. I took a bit of a tumble this morning. I was upstairs when the postman rang, and you know what they are, no one has any patience nowadays, and so I came running down and slipped on the bottom step." She sat on the sofa and put her left foot on a cushion and stroked it. The ankle looked bruised and puffy. Laura wondered if she had been wearing high heels when she fell and decided not to ask, though she knew it was the first question her mother would put when she told her.

Gran said, "No need to tell your mother, mind. I'll be right as a trivet tomorrow."

"Shall I make you a cup of tea?"

"Bless you, chick. No, I'm not paralyzed. But you could find my glasses—let me see, where did I put them?"

"On the stool," Laura said. "With the newspaper."

Her grandmother put her spectacles on and looked at the pamphlet. "Ha!" she said. "Holy rollers."

"What's that?"

"Who are they, is what you mean. People who throw themselves about when the spirit of the Lord seizes them. Not to my taste, though I daresay it livens things up a bit. Go and take a look, why don't you? A bit of religion won't hurt you, any kind better than none. Though don't tell your mother I said that."

Laura groaned. "Oh, Gran, you are *silly*. But I'll have to tell her you've hurt yourself. She'll be mad at *me* if I don't."

Her grandmother looked sulky.

Laura said, "I mean, she'll want to know about shopping, things like that."

"Oh, pish and tush," her grandmother said. "I've got food in the house and I can look after myself. The only thing I can't do is get a shoe on, so I can't look in on old Mrs. Angel. Not that she's helpless, either, but she gets a bit down in the mouth if I don't go to see her. It's not much of a life, stuck in that room. I think how I'd feel if that happened to me, so I try to be regular."

"Alex says she's pretty boring," Laura said, to pay her grandmother back for taking Alex, not her, on these visits.

"Now don't make things up, miss. Alex is very fond of her. I often think it's quite charming to see them together. People say old and young don't mix but I think that's nonsense."

No good arguing with Gran, Laura thought. She said, "Why is Mrs. Angel so lonely? Doesn't she have any other friends?"

"She's a sad woman, that's why. No one likes sad people. Laugh and the world laughs with you, weep and you weep alone. I try to get her to talk about happier days when her husband was still alive and her daughter lived with her."

"Did the daughter die too?"

"No one knows. She disappeared. Walked out one morning twelve years ago to go to the hospital where she worked, on the children's ward, and never came back. Not a word from her since. Poor Angel's still grieving. That's why I take Alex to see her." She smiled, a happy, sly smile, and her eyes gleamed with mischief. "There's a reason why she should take an interest in him, but it's all a bit delicate, so it's no good you asking questions."

"I wasn't going to," Laura said.

Her grandmother sniffed. "Oh, I know you, Miss Nosey Parker. Just like your mother at your age; why, why, why, all the time."

Offended, Laura jutted out her chin and said nothing.

"Not that I blame you," her grandmother said. "It's the only way to find out. Have a chocolate."

"No thank you," Laura said coldly. "It might spoil my supper. If there's nothing you want me to do, I'll go now. I expect Mum will be over later to see you're all right."

"There's no need, dear. I've got a friend coming as a matter of fact. We've spoken once or twice on the Fields and he rang up this morning, and I thought, well, why not, two lonely old people. Of course, that was before I had my silly fall. . . ."

Laura knew what she was expected to say. No, Gran, you're not old. How old is he? What's he like? What's his name? Where does he live?

Well, she wouldn't ask. Not one single question! She said, "I hope you have a nice time."

As she left the house, she remembered Mrs. Angel's drawn curtains and wondered if she ought to have told her grandmother. Should she go back? Gran had called her *nosey* already!

She went down the steps to take another look at the

window; then saw that there was a woman standing outside Mrs. Angel's front door. She had her purse open and a key in her hand. She looked down at Laura with round eyes like small, angry buttons. She said, "What are you staring at? I saw you come out of next door. Has *she* sent you spying?"

Laura gasped. Oh, it wasn't fair! She stuck her tongue out, made a rude noise with her lips, and ran, boiling with rage and with shame.

As she ran past the tent she could hear the singing. *Jesus loves me, this I know, for the Bible tells me so.* She ran straight into Alex and almost sent him flying. He said, "D'you want to go in the tent? Anyone can go. There's a huge lot of people."

She didn't want to go home yet; she felt far too miserable. Perhaps she *was* nosey. Perhaps Mum would find out that she had been rude to that foul, beastly woman. If she went into the tent and sang with the congregation, she could forget all about it, pretend that she'd been there singing and praising the Lord all the time. She took Alex's hand and they went into the tent and stood at the back.

The hymn had finished. The man who had given her the pamphlet was standing on the platform, arms spread out, eyes lifted to the roof of the tent. "Dear Lord," he was saying, "hear our prayers and our singing. Enter us with Thy spirit so we may speak with tongues. Guide us into Thy glory."

Alex nudged her and giggled. She whispered

fiercely, "Don't laugh. This is the same thing as being in church."

It was nicer, she thought, than the church she sometimes went to with Gran. Everyone seemed much more cheerful, smiling happily and clasping each other's hands. "Help us, Lord," the tall preacher said, "with our special prayers for our brothers and sisters who are stricken with illness and pain."

"Rose Simmons needs Thy help, Lord," a woman cried out. She was standing in the aisle, rocking backward and forward. "Rose needs Thy strength to sustain her in her last hours in Saint Emmanuel's Hospice."

"Rose, Rose Simmons," several voices repeated, half groaning, half singing, and then the preacher silenced them with his uplifted hands. "We thank You, Lord, for Rose's life, and if it is Thy will, her peaceful end."

Other names were called out and taken up by the preacher, the congregation swaying like a forest of blown trees as they prayed for recovery for sick friends and relations, or comfort for families who had just lost a loved one. Laura began to feel immensely excited. Longing to join in, she wondered if she should pray for her grandmother, but perhaps a twisted ankle wasn't serious enough to mention. Then a man moved into the aisle, and called out in a strong voice, "Lord, help me to find my son, Winston, who vanished from home fifteen months ago; fill him with Thy spirit and send him home to his sorrowing mother." A woman nearby began to weep noisily. "Winston, ah, my boy Winston, let the Lord enter you," and a kind of deep, hushed, reverent sigh rose in the tent as an accompaniment to her sobbing. Laura looked at Alex and saw he had gone as white as his judo suit. She whispered, "Do you really think they can find people this way?" and he shivered and pressed close against her.

Then, as if in answer, a girl began to moan, "Lord Jesus, find our brother Winston as You found me last year, deep in my wickedness, and brought me home in Thy Glory." She stumbled into the aisle and fell. She lay, jerking and kicking on the ground, her skirt caught between her knees, showing her underwear. A woman bent to pull her skirt down and the preacher thundered, "Leave her be, let her lie where Jesus flung her," and the people lifted their arms and cried, "Praise the Lord."

"I want to go," Alex said. He was clutching himself. "I want to go to the bathroom."

"You would," Laura said. "Just when it's getting interesting."

"I'm sorry."

"Never *mind*. Come on, you can't help it."

They were singing again now, a rousing rollicking tune unlike any hymn Laura knew. As they slipped out of the tent into the evening sunlight, the tent seemed to heave—straining at the guy ropes as if the singing were billowing it up like in a wind. Alex blinked, his color returning. He said, "It's going off. I don't think I need the bathroom anymore, I was just frightened."

"What of?"

"I don't know. It was so . . ."

He shook his head, unable to think of the word that he wanted. Laura said, "It's just like any church, really, people asking for things. I mean, in the Catholic Church there are special saints that you pray to when you want to find something. My friend, Carla—she's Catholic—she lost her best pen and she prayed to Saint Anthony and found it in her desk at school the next morning."

"I expect it was there all the time," Alex said. "I don't believe it. Do you believe it, Laura?"

"I'm not sure. You couldn't be *sure* unless you'd asked for something yourself and you found it. Something, or *someone*. If someone you knew disappeared."

He gave a little sigh. She looked at his face and saw it closed and secret as if a curtain had been drawn across it. She thought of Mrs. Angel and her closed curtains and looked across the Fields. An ambulance was parked outside the terrace, blue lights flashing. She couldn't see Mrs. Angel's front door because the ambulance hid it, but she could see her grandmother's. And Gran was there, leaning on a stick, slowly hobbling down the steps. Laura grabbed Alex's arm and said, "We've got to get Mum. I think something awful has happened."

Chapter Three

Alex stood at the window of his room. The big tent, empty now, was ghost pale in the darkness; the tall trees around the edge of the Upper Field, black against the pink night sky of London. Their leafless branches were like twisted, skinny arms, Alex thought. He had turned the light off in his room so that no one could see him standing there, watching the houses on the other side of the Fields. Watching, and waiting.

Mrs. Angel's house was dark. They had taken her away in the ambulance and Dad had driven his grandmother to see her in the hospital. Mrs. Angel was very ill, his mother had told him. When he had asked what had happened her face had been grave. No one knew. Mrs. Fowles had found her unconscious on the floor by her chair. She must have lain there a long time, helpless, alone. "Poor soul," his mother had said.

But she hadn't been alone last night, Alex knew. Mr. Fowles had been there; he had drawn the curtains, and Alex had seen him. But he hadn't told anyone. He had gone downstairs to have supper with his mother and father and Laura, a special late supper for his Finding Day after the little ones were in bed, with candles on the table and everyone laughing and happy.

He should have told someone, Alex thought now. But what could he have said? That Mrs. Angel's nephew had come to see her? Nothing in that. He had drawn the curtains, but people often did that in the evening. Mr. Fowles had been rude to his grandmother, a "dreadful man" Gran had called him, but that didn't mean he was wicked, that he would harm an old woman. All the same, Alex was frightened. He wished Dad would come home. That is, half of him wished it. The other half was scared, not wanting to know.

He thought—if he had known she was ill, he could have asked God to help her when he and Laura had been in the tent. It wasn't his fault that he hadn't known, but it felt like his fault. He wished Laura would come, or his mother. He leaned his forehead against the cold glass of the window and sighed. He was beginning to feel very sleepy.

Lights flashed in his eyes as a car turned off the road between the Upper and Lower Fields into the drive outside the house. The car stopped and his father got out. Alex looked at his grandmother's house and saw the lights on. Dad must have taken her home already and Alex had been too sleepy to notice. Wide awake suddenly, he shot across the room to his bed and dived under the covers. The feeling of half wanting to know what had happened and half not wanting was making him feel cold and sick. He heard his father's voice, then his steps climbing the stairs. The bathroom door closed. Alex heard the lavatory flush, the bathroom door opening. He called softly, "Dad . . ." half hoping that Dad wouldn't hear him.

Light came in from the landing. Dad said, "Alex?"

"Mmm . . ." Alex sat up, yawning, rubbing his eyes, pretending he had just woken up.

Dad said, "All right, love? Do you want something?"

"Glass of water. I'm thirsty."

His father went to the bathroom and came back. He sat on the edge of the bed while Alex drank. He took the empty glass. Alex said slowly, fearfully, "Is she all right, Dad? Mrs. Angel?"

"Well. Not *all right*, really, but she's tucked up in bed and quite comfortable. She woke up while we were there and was able to talk to your grandmother."

"Is she going to die?"

"She's very ill, Alex."

"Did she fall off her chair? Did she hurt herself?"

"There's a bruise on her forehead. But that's nothing, really. Her heart's very weak. She shouldn't have been living alone."

"*He* was there," Alex said. "Her nephew, that man, Mr. Fowles. Gran and I met him yesterday evening; he was going to see her. When I got home, I could see them both in the room."

"Yes?" Dad waited. "What happened, Alex?"

"Nothing, really. He just drew the curtains."

His father smiled. "If that's all, why are you worried? Because you didn't tell someone? Not much to tell, was there? Just that her nephew was visiting."

"I don't know," Alex said.

His father was quiet for a minute. Then he said, "Was it something your grandmother said?"

"She doesn't like Mr. Fowles."

"That was apparent this evening." Dad cleared his throat, the way he did when he had something awkward to say. "He was there at the hospital. He said his aunt was all right when he left her. He had offered to help her to bed but she wouldn't let him. Then there was a bit of a shouting match between him and your Gran. You came into it, Alex, which is why I am telling you." He stopped and frowned, as if wondering how to go on. He said, uncertainly, "You're a bit young for this. But things have been said, and I have to ask you. Gran has taken you to see Mrs. Angel quite a lot, hasn't she? Has she ever said, well, that there was a particular reason? That you ought to be especially nice to the old lady? Anything like that?"

"I don't understand."

"No. Of course you don't. Well."

"Gran did say—it was my Finding Day—Mrs. Angel might give me a present."

"That's all?"

Alex burst out, "I just tried to be nice because Gran said she was lonely. I didn't like going." He wished he could explain how he'd felt, that it was as if *he* were a present, a bunch of flowers or a box of chocolates that Gran was taking to cheer up her sick friend, but it sounded silly. Vain, too, as if he thought he was such a nice boy that any old lady would be delighted to see him.

That's what Laura would say if he told her.

His father laughed and put his arms around him. "Poor Alex. Never mind; you're a kind boy. Extra kind, if you didn't want to go, really."

Alex mumbled, against his father's broad chest, "She did give me things sometimes. A pear, or a sweet. Once she gave me a pound." He wondered if he should tell Dad about the photograph. But Gran hadn't wanted his mother to know. Perhaps she had thought Mum would say it was a silly present. And he had already been mean enough to old Mrs. Angel, telling his father he hadn't wanted to visit her. And there was something else, too; something creepy about the way Gran had gone on about the girl in the photograph, about her looking like Alex, or Alex looking like her, that had made him hot and uncomfortable. He felt hot now, remembering. He said, "I never asked her for anything. Honest."

"I'm sure you didn't." Dad drew the bedclothes up around his shoulders and kissed him. "Forget all about it now. Go to sleep."

"I can't," Alex said. "My mind's buzzing."

"Count sheep jumping over a gate. That's supposed to help."

"It wouldn't help if you were a farmer. You might think you'd lost one."

"I never thought of that. Smart boy! Talk if you want to."

Alex said, "Gran says Mr. Fowles is only after one

thing. I asked her what she meant but she didn't explain."

"I expect . . . I expect she just meant that he didn't care for Mrs. Angel as she does. That may be true. Your grandmother is a warm, loving woman, if a bit fanciful. She likes making up stories."

"You tell me a story," Alex said. "Then I might go to sleep."

"That's not very flattering," his father said. But there was a smile in his voice. "What kind of story?"

"About when I was born," Alex said. "My Birth Day. I know you don't know, but you could make something up."

"I wish I could, Alex. Does it matter so much?"

"No. It was just something Gran said at my party."

His father muttered something. It sounded like *Damn the woman* and Alex was surprised, because his father never swore. Then he said, "You're a nice boy, so whoever your real parents were, they must have been nice people, too. Only for some reason they couldn't look after you. That was sad for them but lucky for us."

It didn't make much of a story, Alex thought. He said, "It would be more interesting if my real Dad was a pirate, and my mother was a princess that the pirates had captured. It would be unlucky to keep a baby on a pirate ship, so they sailed up the Thames and left me with the Sphinx."

"It must be a long time since there has been a pirate ship on the Thames," his father said gravely. "Still, anything's possible!"

Alex said, "They won't ever come back for me, will they?" This frightened him suddenly. "You wouldn't let them take me away."

"No. You're not scared of that, are you?"

"I don't think so. It's just something I thought of." But it did scare him a little, thinking of pirates with cutlasses in their teeth climbing in through his window. He said, "It's all right. I'm quite sleepy now." He closed his eyes and tried to count sheep and it seemed to work after all because when he had counted to twenty-four he felt himself drifting. The twenty-fifth sheep pulled a face at him as Laura did sometimes; a white, woolly sheep, jumping a gate, changing, becoming Laura; and the next sheep had a human face too, a girl's face with dark eyes that grew larger and larger, like black pools of water. "You could drown in them," he said, the words too smudgy and blurred for his father to hear, and turned on his side, cuddling into his pillow.

He slept soundly the rest of that night. He was asleep when Mrs. Angel died in the hospital. He slept through the sound of the telephone ringing in the early morning and would have slept on, missing breakfast, if his mother had not come to wake him.

And when he did wake, the world had changed for him.

Chapter Four

Laura knew what had happened before Alex did. She was more interested in what grown-ups were talking about, partly because she was older and partly because she was afraid that they might be saying unpleasant things about her.

So she kept her ears open. If she pretended to be watching television or reading a book, no one ever seemed to suspect she was listening. Even if what she heard seemed a bit dull to start with, there was always a chance that it might turn out to be useful later. It wasn't like spying, she thought, more like doing a jigsaw. You plodded on, fitting bits of blue sky or green grass together and then found a foot or an arm or the nose that belonged to the face that made the important part of the picture.

She knew, early on, that her grandmother had wanted to take Alex with her to Mrs. Angel's funeral and that her mother had refused to allow it. Alex was "too young." It was "unnecessary." It would "only cause trouble."

Although Laura had wondered what kind of "trouble," she hadn't paid much attention. It was just part of the old, boring argument between her mother and grandmother. Her mother was jealous because Gran made a fuss of Alex and liked to take him out and show him off to her friends. In the week after the funeral Laura only went on listening out of habit and because she was always excited when Mum and Gran quarreled. She liked a good quarrel herself and she had the feeling that however angry they sounded, they rather enjoyed it.

One quarrel, about a month after Mrs. Angel had died, was more fierce and alarming than usual. Alex was out on the Fields playing with Bob and Ellie, and from her room where she was sitting at her desk and doing her homework, Laura could hear what was being said in the kitchen.

She heard her mother's voice, trying—or pretending to try—to be patient. "I know you say she was fond of him, Ma. But Mr. Fowles had looked after her all these years. He had a right to *some* expectations, and if he chooses to make a fuss it could be very unpleasant. For you as much as for anyone. That's one of the things George is worried about. The point is, George says, what the lawyers will want to know— whether there was any excessive persuasion."

"George" was Laura's father. Sometimes, when Laura's mother wanted to say something unpleasant, she pretended that he had said it first. *Dad says he's afraid you aren't working hard enough, you had such a bad math report last term*, she had said today when Laura had asked if she could go to the cinema with Carla and two boys in their class. Which was why Laura was sitting at her desk now with her algebra textbook propped up in front of her. She wondered if her mother had forgotten she was in the house. Serve her right if she has, Laura thought. She got up and went to the door.

Her grandmother said, "Persuasion, persuasion—what do you mean? Poor Angel wanted to do something for Alex. What's wrong with that, may I ask? Why does it upset you that he should have this piece of good luck? Do you resent it, is that it?"

"Don't be silly, Ma, please. Though of course it does seem unfair on the others."

"So you *do* resent it! Poor little chap! Poor little orphan!"

"He's not an orphan, Ma." Laura heard her mother's voice more angry now: furious, on the edge of tears. She crept a little way down the stairs. Her mother said, spacing her words out deliberately, controlling her anger, "Alex is our son, our child, like the others."

"Blood is thicker than water," Gran said.

"That's a ridiculous thing to say and you know it. If this had happened to Laura, or to Bob, or to Ellie, I would feel the same way. Don't you understand the trouble this is going to make in the family?"

"George will know how to handle it," Gran said. "He's a sensible man. More sense in his little finger than you have in your whole body. He loves the boy."

"You think I don't? Oh, how *can* you!"

"I didn't say that. Just that you think more about things being equal and fair than you should. That's what will cause trouble if anything does. Nothing is fair in this life, my girl; none of your children are *equal*. Laura is more clever than Alex by a long chalk. That's not fair in your book, is it? Why don't you lop off a bit of her brain to put matters right? That's no sillier than wanting to deny Alex this little windfall."

Laura's mother began to laugh. She laughed with little screams and whoops, not happily, Laura thought, but as if she were being tickled. Laura ran the rest of the way down the stairs and stood in the open doorway. She saw her mother's face, round and red as a winter sun, with a dark, open laughing mouth in the middle. Her mother said, "A *little windfall*, Ma! Is that how you think of it? As if she'd left him a few pence for his piggy bank?" Then she saw Laura. Her hand went to her mouth.

Laura thought—She'll be angry with me for listening. She started to talk very fast with a babyish whine, pretending to be scared about something else, something childish and silly. "Mum, you won't lop a bit off my brain, promise me you won't. I'm sorry, I couldn't help hearing. I had to go to the bathroom and you were both shouting."

She saw her grandmother's knowing smile, her raised eyebrows, and knew that she understood what Laura was up to. But her mother was taken in. She said, "Laura, oh my poor pet, of course not." She turned on her mother. "See what you've done, you've frightened the child."

"Codswallop," Gran said. "Laura doesn't frighten that easily."

Laura was indignant. "It's not a nice thing to hear, Gran. *You* wouldn't like it." Then she remembered that her grandmother had said she was clever. She accused her mother instead. "It's not my fault that I'm here. You stopped me going out. I had a bad math report last term because I'd been put up in the top stream and hadn't done all the work, and you knew that. You just didn't want me to go out with Carla."

"You're too young to be hanging about with boys," her mother said—as if Jimmy and Fred were *apes*, Laura thought suddenly—seeing them in her mind's eye, hanging about in the trees, swinging long-armed through the branches, scratching their armpits and chattering.

"She's getting to the age," Gran said. "If she can't be open about it, she'll be off on the sly."

"Don't tell me how to bring up my children, please," Laura's mother said wearily. Then, to Laura, "You shouldn't eavesdrop on other people's conversation, but it's not your fault this time. I was upset. I forgot you were here. I don't know how much you heard."

"Most of it. I suppose you think I ought to keep *plugs* in my ears! How much did Mrs. Angel leave Alex?"

"Trust you to ask that, miss!" her grandmother said.

"I don't see why not," her mother said. She looked gravely at Laura. "You can keep a secret, I hope. Your father and I don't want Alex to know anything yet. He's only a little boy. It would only unsettle him. So you must promise me."

Laura nodded impatiently. "Is he going to be *rich*?"

Her mother sighed. "I'm afraid so. *How* rich depends on what happens. Mrs. Angel left everything— her money, the house, and everything in it—divided between her daughter and Alex. But no one knows where the daughter is. She may even be dead. If she doesn't turn up in the next four months, if the lawyers can't trace her, it all goes to Alex. Do you understand?"

"Of course. I'm not stupid. But I don't understand *why*. I mean, why she left Alex anything. He's not a relation."

"That's a question I'd like to have answered," her mother said, rather grimly.

"Gran knows," Laura said. She looked at her grandmother. "You said there was a reason why Mrs. Angel should take an interest in Alex. You told me . . ."

"Did I, dear?" Gran shook her head wonderingly. "I can't say I remember. I may have said she was fond of him."

Laura said, "It's not fair."

"I was afraid you'd feel that," her mother said. "I'm sorry, Laura."

Laura said, "I don't mean about the money. I mean it's unfair not to tell him. Keeping it secret! If I was Alex, I'd want to know. I'd be *furious*. . . ."

"He will know," her mother said. "When your father and I decide the time's right. But that isn't now. Be a good girl, try and put it out of your mind. It really isn't important. Money isn't important. The important thing is that you should all work hard and do well. Have you finished your homework?"

"*Homework,*" Laura said in a disgusted voice. "*Homework!* I couldn't. I'd *burst.*"

Her mother looked tired. She sank down on a chair and leaned her elbows on the table. She said, "All right, darling. . . ."

It was far from all right, Laura thought. Her mother had tried to sound calm, but she wasn't calm underneath. She said, "Soon as I go, you and Gran will start quarreling."

"No, we won't." Her mother smiled at her weakly. "I promise. And you promise about Alex, won't you? I know you'll be sensible."

This wasn't worth answering. Laura looked at the clock on the wall. "It's almost suppertime. What's for supper?"

"I don't know. I haven't thought . . ."

Gran said sharply, "Can't you see, your poor mother's worn out. Supper will be when it's ready. Meantime, I'm going to make her a good cup of tea." She stood up and hobbled to the stove. Her ankle was bandaged and she was wearing flat shoes. They made her look smaller, and older.

Mum said, "Laura, darling, it's time Bob and Ellie came home. They can bathe before supper. Will you fetch them?"

Laura said, "You always say Laura *darling* when you want to get rid of me."

She stomped down the hall, past the stacked bicycles and Ellie's old baby buggy, and paused before the open front door to listen. But all she heard was her mother saying, "Let's have China tea, Ma. You like China, don't you? There's a new packet, on the right, in the cupboard."

Chapter Five

As Laura crossed the Upper Field, Bob and Ellie came racing toward her. Bob was six and Ellie was five; she tried to keep up with her brother but her legs were much shorter. "Wait," she was panting. "Wait for me, *wait*." Bob reached back for her hand and pulled her along and she squealed, "Oh Bob, my feet's flying."

"You'll pull her over," Laura said as they reached her. They both laughed, eyes bright, cheeks scarlet with running.

"Alex wants you," Bob said. "He sent us home and he said, tell Laura to come. He's over by Gran's house; we was playing, and then the man come."

"What man?" Laura said, but they had run off, hand in hand. Laura watched them stop at the drive between their house and the Field, looking both ways before they crossed it. Bob opened the front door with the key that he kept hanging around his neck on a leather thong.

"Six years old is too young for a key," Laura grumbled out loud. *She* hadn't been given a key until she was ten. "Bob is such a sensible boy," her mother had said when Laura had pointed this out, as if Laura had not been sensible at that age, and Laura felt the unfairness burn hotly inside her. Mum was always on about things being fair, but she wasn't fair herself, was she? It wasn't fair to make her keep a secret from Alex, particularly when it was something so interesting. It was making her tell a lie. In a way, Laura thought indignantly, turning her into a cheat and a liar!

She couldn't see Alex at first. There was a small van parked outside Mrs. Angel's house. Her front door was open and, as Laura approached, a man came down the steps carrying a big cardboard box. She saw the raised white scar on his cheek. He put the box in the back of the van and ran back up the steps. A woman appeared at the front door with another box that he took from her. "Careful," she called, as he hurried to the van, "some of those things are breakable." She was the woman with small, angry eyes who had called Laura a spy.

Laura saw Alex. He was crouching—*hiding*—between two parked cars a little way up the road from the van. She went up behind him and hissed, "What are you doing?"

"Sssh. Be quiet, Laura, he'll see me."

"Who are they?"

"Mr. Fowles. She's his wife, I expect. He's horrible. He saw me with Bob and Ellie and he told me to clear off. He was *nasty*."

His lips trembled. "Oh, don't be a baby," Laura

said, but she put an arm around him. She could feel him shaking. She said, "People are nasty sometimes; you have to get used to it."

He said sorrowfully, "They're taking Mrs. Angel's things. I think it's awful."

"They're not burglars. I mean, we know who they are."

"It's not that. Its just, she's only just *dead* . . ." He choked on a sob.

Laura said, "Then it doesn't matter to her. Nor to you." She removed her arm from his shoulder. "After all, you didn't like her much, did you?"

"I didn't *not* like her." He screwed his eyes up, trying to think what he meant and explain it. "I didn't like going there all the time. Gran *making* me go. That's not the same thing. But she liked all her pretty things, and they're bundling them up and taking them; they don't *care*." His wide, dark eyes looked at her sadly. He said, in an awed voice, "Gran will be mad when she knows."

"It isn't Gran's business. They're not her things, are they?"

But they didn't belong to Mr. Fowles, either. Mrs. Angel had left them to her daughter, to Alex. Fending off the uncomfortable feeling this gave her, Laura said, "I expect they do care that she's dead. After all, they are her relations."

"I know," Alex said. "We ought to say that we're sorry. I was going to, but then he shouted, and I forgot."

At this moment Mr. Fowles closed the van doors. His wife came out of Mrs. Angel's house and slammed the front door. She came down the steps and got into the passenger seat of the van. Mr. Fowles stood beside it, looking up and down the street. "Duck down," Laura whispered. "Keep still."

She wasn't sure why she was scared. She and Alex had only been watching. Then she thought, *spying*, and felt her head spin. When Alex stood up and marched boldly out of their hiding place, she thought she would faint. But she knew she must follow him. Although Alex sometimes seemed timid, it was only because he hated it when people were rude or unkind to him. Once he made up his mind that he ought to do something he was always brave.

She kept her distance behind him as he marched up to Mr. Fowles, hearing him say loudly, if a bit breathlessly, "I'm very sorry about your aunt, Mr. Fowles."

Mr. Fowles looked amazed. He gave an odd sort of laugh with no humor in it. "That's rich," he said. "Coming from you."

"But I am sorry," Alex said. "I'm sure you must be very unhappy."

"Unhappy?" Mr. Fowles said. "Unhappy?" He spoke slowly and thoughtfully as if he were turning the word over in his mind to make sure of its meaning. Then he gave another strange barking laugh. "I daresay I am, though I'd put it stronger. And not quite in the way that you mean. Never mind. My wife and I have been collecting a few mementos to keep the old girl's memory green. It's not quite what we might have expected but there's no justice, is there?"

"I don't know what you mean, Mr. Fowles." Alex sounded politely puzzled. Quaking, Laura moved closer, standing beside him, touching his arm to let him know she was there to protect him.

"Don't you now?" Mr. Fowles said. "Well, of course you're the lucky one, aren't you? Pretty pleased with yourself, I don't doubt. Cock-a-hoop."

All the time he was saying this he was smiling, his harelip stretched shinily, his eyes glistening at both Alex and Laura. She said, "Alex only wanted to say he was sorry."

"So he should be. If he doesn't know why, he can ask his grandmother. She's a wicked old woman, taking advantage of a poor soul whose wits were wandering, turning her away from her own flesh and blood. But you can tell her from me she's not heard the last of it. Eric Fowles is not a man to sit back and say nothing."

There was a soapy dribble of spit on his mouth. Alex whispered, "Let's go home, Laura."

She pushed him behind her. She shouted, "My Gran isn't wicked. Mrs. Angel was her best *friend*. She was sorry for her because she was lonely. And . . . and . . . you shouldn't have been taking those things away. They don't belong to you. That was *stealing* . . ."

She was so angry, the words seemed to fly out of her mouth like black birds. And then she was frightened. She grabbed Alex's hand and ran—fear thudding in her chest and in her head—terrified that Mr. Fowles would chase after them, shouting and swearing.

Halfway across the Fields she had to stop, gasping with a sudden stitch in her side, and looked back. The van was being driven away, brakes squealing as it turned the corner by the mailbox. "Oh," she said, "*Alex*. Why on earth did you *speak* to him?"

"I didn't say anything wrong. *You* shouldn't have said that about stealing. He might tell the police."

"He won't do that, dummy."

She looked at his bewildered and innocent face. Of course, he understood nothing. She understood more; like bits of a jigsaw, some of the things she had heard began to fall into place. Mr. Fowles had expected Mrs. Angel to leave her money to him, but her grandmother had persuaded her friend to "do something" for Alex. Exactly why and how she didn't know—that was a missing part of the jigsaw—but she could make a good guess. She said, "Oh, Alex, if only you weren't so sweet, always."

"I'm not sweet." In protest he thumped her in the chest. It was only a little thump but it enraged her.

"You mustn't hit girls in the chest; you might give them cancer."

"I didn't hit hard, don't be silly. Just don't call me *sweet*. It's so soppy." His face creased with anxiety. "Why was he so cross? I mean, of course he was cross when you said he'd been stealing, but he was cross before that. I know he doesn't like Gran. Why did he say I was lucky?"

She couldn't explain. She had promised not to. She said, "I don't know. He's just a nasty man, that's all. I *told* you, some people are nasty."

Chapter Six

Alex had been twice around the Fields on his
roller boots without falling over. On this third
round he saw his grandmother sitting with a strange
man on one of the benches. As he braked neatly in
front of her she said, "Alex, dear, I want you to meet
Major Bumpus."

Major Bumpus had fierce, blue eyes and a stiff
brown moustache. When Alex said, "How do you do,
sir?" he nodded approvingly.

"Glad to make your acquaintance. Heard a lot
about you from your grandmother. Handsome lad,
Amy."

Embarrassed, Alex did the splits, quite elegantly,
but hurting his thighs. He said, "Ouch," and laughed.

"Don't show off, dear," his grandmother said. "You
might injure yourself."

She was looking very pretty, Alex thought. He said,
"I like your dress, Gran. I'm glad your leg's better."

"Not quite right yet," Major Bumpus said. "No
more fancy heels for a bit. Good thing, too. You know

what they say? Most ladies' shoes are made by fellers who have heard of a foot but never seen one. Not like those fine boots you've got there. Lucky feller. Lucky in more ways than one, so I'm told."

Gran said, rather quickly, "Now, Monty!"

"Ah," Major Bumpus said. "Harrumph. Shooting my mouth off. Sorry, Amy." His eyes twinkled at Alex. "Well. Young feller-me-lad. What are you going to do with yourself when you grow up? Train for the Olympics? Quite a nifty skater already. Apart from that, what's your game? Rugger?"

"I don't like football," Alex said. "Dad says it's because I'm small for my age and always getting knocked over, but I think I just like things I can do on my own, like swimming and skating and judo." He added, "I'm sorry," because most people seemed to think this was odd.

"Why *sorry*?" Major Bumpus said. "No point in running about after balls if you don't enjoy it. You stick to your guns. Tell the truth and shame the devil."

"Oh, he's always been an honest boy," Gran said proudly.

They both smiled at him. Alex decided he liked Major Bumpus. But he felt suddenly shy. He said, "I'd better go home now."

He skated off extra fast because he knew they were watching him, the roller boots making a lovely, gritty sound on the tarmac path and the wind lifting his hair, making his cheeks burn. When he got to the drive in front of his house he went straight across without looking, and a motorbike swerved, hooting and screeching behind him. The rider shouted, "Bloody young half-wit!"

Safe indoors, unfastening his roller boots in the hall, his ears were on fire, like his cheeks. He heard his mother typing in the small room at the back that she used as a study and felt weak with relief. If she'd been in the front living room, she would have heard the bike and looked through the window. He opened the study door and said, in an innocent voice, "Hallo, Mum."

She looked at him vaguely. "What is it, Alex? I'm terribly busy."

"Can I help, Mum?"

She shook her head. "It's just letters and bills. Half an hour, darling. Close the door, will you?"

He closed the door. He went upstairs. Bob and Ellie were in the room that they shared: Bob on his back on the floor with his sweater pulled up, Ellie holding a toy stethoscope to his bare stomach. She was saying, "You're having a baby, Bob. I can hear its heart beating." As Alex came in they both screwed their heads around and looked at him crossly. Ellie said, "Go away, Alex, we're playing doctors."

"All right," Alex said. "I'm not interfering."

Sometimes they played doctors for hours. Last week it had been chicken pox; they had had a packet of joke scabs that they stuck all over their faces. This week it was babies. A teacher at their school was having a baby and Alex guessed, because the same thing had happened to his teacher when he had been young, that she had been drawing pictures on the blackboard, showing her class how babies grew. Alex remembered coming home and looking at his stomach in the mirror, sticking it out and pretending. Laura had laughed at him and made him angry. It still seemed unfair to him that boys couldn't have babies. He wondered if Bob knew that he couldn't, and if he ought to have told him in case someone should laugh at him for not knowing.

Ask Laura, he thought. She was too old and sensible, now, to laugh at a little boy, and would know how to explain to Bob better than he would.

But when he pushed her door open, she wasn't alone. Carla was there. They were sitting on the bed, red-faced and giggling.

Laura said crossly, "Alex, why don't you *knock*?"

"Boys ought to knock before they come into a girl's room," Carla said, and giggled again. She was a fat girl with a puffy white face, and when she giggled, spit flew. "They might see something they shouldn't."

Laura wiped her cheek where the spit had landed and rolled her eyes at Alex. Although Carla was supposed to be her best friend, Laura often found her embarrassing. In fact, she only put up with her because Carla's parents allowed her to give parties in their house when they were out, and Laura was afraid of not being invited. Alex, who knew this because Laura had told him, was not surprised when she said, "Go away, Alex. We're talking in private."

Carla wriggled her plump shoulders and laughed. More spit sprayed the air around her. She said, "Don't send him off, Laura. You know I like Alex. You like *me*, Alex, don't you?"

She winked at him. He was astonished. Carla, who had no brothers and sisters, usually behaved as if he were invisible, barging straight past if they met on the stairs, only saying, "Hi, there," in a bored voice if he spoke to her first.

"Shut up," Laura said. "Leave him alone, Carla."

Carla pouted. "Don't be mean. I'm your best friend, aren't I?" She was only playing at being offended. Her eyes, the pale green of gooseberries, were laughing and sly.

"Don't be silly." Laura's face had turned scarlet. She said, "He's too young for you, anyway."

"Oh, I don't know," Carla said. "Girls often marry younger men, don't they? I know Alex and I are both too young at the moment, but we could have a secret engagement." She batted her eyelids—thick, fair lashes fluttering. "I'd like a rich husband."

Laura put her hands over her ears. She bent over, bent double, forehead almost touching her knees. "Stop it. *Stop it!* I'll never tell you anything again, ever. . . ."

Carla sniggered. The snigger turned into a giggle and then into a kind of fit. She giggled and snorted and yelped as if she couldn't help it, as if something so extraordinarily funny had happened that she had lost all control. She collapsed on her back on the bed, waving her legs about. Her thighs and her bottom were tight as drums in her jeans. She gasped, through her snorts and her yelps and her giggles, "We c-could have a yacht, and a p-private airplane, and a Rolls-Royce c-car, and we could live at the Ritz."

Mad, Alex thought. *Raving. Bonkers.* He saw that Laura had lifted her head and was looking at him in despair. *Serves her right for making a best friend of such an idiot.* All the same, Alex was sorry for Laura. He pulled a comical face to cheer her up, spreading his mouth wide with his thumbs and pulling his eyes down at the corners with his forefingers. When she didn't laugh, he said, "What's she on about?"

Laura shook her head from side to side, very slowly and miserably. She whispered, "Nothing. Really, it's nothing; just a silly joke. Please go away, Alex. I'm sorry. . . ."

"Doesn't he know?" In spite of her noisy giggling and leg waving act, Carla had heard what Laura had said. She sat up at once and said, speaking quite normally, "Pardon *me*! If he doesn't *know*, then it's me that ought to say sorry! I didn't know it was a huge secret. You didn't say, did you, Laura?"

"I was going to. I just didn't have time." Laura caught her breath, suddenly glaring at Alex. "It was all your fault, bursting in. Now I shall get into terrible trouble. Mum will just *hate* me." She started to cry. "I won't ever forgive you."

"Why? What *for*? What don't I know?"

Carla was off the bed, coming toward him. A strong, big girl, towering over him. She put her hands on his shoulders, twisted him around, and marched him out of the room. She hissed, "See what you've done, little beast," and slammed the door in his face.

Alex ran to his own room, slammed *his* door, and threw himself down on his bed. He stuck his fingers in his ears, hearing the blood boom in his head like the sea in a cave.

He stayed like that for some time. He didn't move when the door opened, not even when someone sat down beside him. A hand touched his hair and he shook his head, burrowing his face deeper into the pillow.

His mother said, "Come on, Alex love, don't be sulky."

"I'm not sulking," he said indignantly, rolling over.

She laughed. "I thought that would budge you."

"I thought you were Laura. I'm angry with Laura."

"Mmm. I was angry as well to begin with. But it was too much to expect, I'm afraid, that she wouldn't tell *someone*. A pity it had to be that frightful girl, for a number of reasons. Still, she was honest enough to come and tell me what happened, and she's very sorry."

Alex didn't understand a word of this. "She said she'd never forgive me. Just for going into her silly old room without knocking."

His mother said, with gentle reproof, "I think it was more than that, wasn't it?"

"No, it wasn't. I didn't do anything else, not a *thing*. I haven't been horrible. It's Laura that's horrible, and her fat pig friend, Carla, laughing at me and pushing me out, it's so *mean*."

He was trying not to cry, struggling with a tight feeling in his chest. He said, with a rasp in his throat, "I really and truly didn't do anything beastly."

"No one has said you did, darling."

In spite of that *darling* she sounded exasperated. But then she sighed and smiled sadly. "Poor Alex, you really don't know what it was all about, do you? Laura thought you must have guessed, but I suppose that was only because she felt guilty. Never mind. It was stupid of me to try and keep it a secret. You were bound to find out sooner or later."

It seemed, from her sighs and sad smiles, that she had something unpleasant to tell him. When she had finished explaining she was still frowning and solemn, and Alex was mystified. If old Mrs. Angel had left him some money, that was something to be pleased about, surely? But his mother's expression made him uneasy.

"It was nice of her, wasn't it?" he ventured at last. Something Mr. Fowles had said rose up in his mind. *Her own flesh and blood.* He said, "I mean, I'm not one of her family."

"She had grown fond of you, I expect," his mother said absently. She gave another of those small, worried sighs as if this answer didn't quite satisfy her. Then she got up from the bed and said, rather more briskly, "Why not, after all? Better you than a cats' home. We must all try not to let it make any difference."

He didn't know what she meant. He felt too shy, for some reason, to ask. What had a cats' home to do with it? A lot of thoughts seemed to be chasing through his head. It was exciting to think he might have some money. He would be able to buy a new bicycle. Laura had had a new one for her birthday last year but there must be something else she would like. Perhaps there would be enough money to buy everyone in the family a special present. He wished he had liked Mrs. Angel more. His grandmother had wanted them to be friends. She had kept on, telling him that Mrs. Angel liked *him;* it was one of the things that had always made him uncomfortable.

He began to wish that his mother would go away and leave him alone to think quietly. But she was moving around the room, tidying, straightening his books on the shelf, putting his clothes away. She picked up his football jersey from a chair and sniffed at it. He said, "It isn't smelly. I've only worn it once," and she opened the bottom drawer of the chest to put it away.

She was bent over, her back to him. He couldn't see what she was doing. She said, "What's this, Alex? *Who* is it?"

She turned. She was holding the photograph Mrs. Angel had given him. He had forgotten he had put it there, in the drawer. She rubbed the glass with her sleeve and held it up to the light.

He said, "It's Mrs. Angel's daughter. Mrs. Angel gave it to me. It was a present for my Finding Day."

He remembered that his grandmother hadn't wanted his mother to see it. But Gran had told Major Bumpus that he was an honest boy. He felt hot and guilty. He said, "Gran said I looked like her, that's why Mrs. Angel gave me the picture. I think that's why, anyway."

His mother looked from the picture to Alex. "Yes," she said. "Yes, I see." She gave a little laugh, as if something embarrassed her. She said, "Trust my old mother! Though I wouldn't have thought she'd have gone *quite* so far!" In spite of her laugh, she was angry. Alex could hear it in her voice, see it in her flushed cheeks, her bright eyes. She said, "What did your dear grandmother say to you? Can you remember?"

Alex shook his head.

"Oh, come *on*! Even you must have seen what she was up to!" Then she seemed to check herself. She smiled at Alex. "No, I don't suppose you did. Why on earth should you?"

But she was still angry. Too angry for Alex to ask what it was he ought to have seen. He said, "Don't be angry, Mum."

"I'm not angry."

"Yes you are." Misery broke over him. "Laura's angry with me, now you're angry, and I haven't done anything. It's not fair."

The tears that he'd held back before came flooding now, drowning his eyes so that his mother's face trembled in front of him. She sat on the bed and put her arms tightly around him. "Hush," she said. "Don't cry. No one's angry with *you*, my poor baby."

And because it was pleasant to be cuddled and loved by his mother, who wasn't in the ordinary way much of a cuddler, Alex tried to believe her.

Chapter Seven

In the next few days, Alex's mother smiled a lot, very brightly. But behind the smiles, she was angry. She snapped at Bob for leaving his scooter on its side in the hall although no one had fallen over it. She sent Ellie to bed in the middle of supper one evening because she spat in her milk. When Laura came home half an hour late from a party at Carla's house, she took her front door key away as a punishment. His turn was next, Alex thought philosophically.

At least when it came he had warning. His friend Willy Tucker had shown him the newspaper. He had telephoned Alex the moment he'd got in from school, before he had spoken to anyone. Willy had said, "Meet me at the shelter, back of the playground. I've got something to show you. Be quick. It's *fantastic.*"

The big mower was cutting the Lower Field, throwing up grass and daisies. When Alex got to the shelter, Willy was waiting. He was so pale with excitement that the freckles on his nose stood out dark as brown pips in a white apple.

They sat on the bench in the shelter, the newspaper between them. The picture was on the front page: a baby in a shawl; a nurse holding it, looking down, smiling. The caption said FOUNDLING COMES INTO A FORTUNE, and beneath it:

> An abandoned baby, found on the Thames Embankment eleven years ago, is the surprise heir to an elderly widow, Mrs. Harriet Ethelberta Angel (81) who died recently of a cerebral hemorrhage. The will is disputed by a nephew, Mr. Eric Fowles, on the grounds that his aunt had been pressurized into making it by a neighbor, who is the boy's grandmother. In a telephone interview, Mr. Fowles said that his aunt was "too old to know what she was doing." Mrs. Angel's attorney has stated, however, that his client was of sound mind when she made this last will. He would not have drawn it up otherwise. We are withholding the boy's name at the attorney's request, but we understand that he was a frequent visitor to Mrs. Angel's residence on Finsbury Fields and that she was very attached to him.

Alex said, "What's it *mean*?"

"You can read, can't you? That's you in the picture. My Mum says she remembers it happening. You being found and all that. There was a lot in the papers and on TV and everything."

"I can't remember that, can I?" Alex said. But he knew, all the same. His mother and father had kept a file of newspaper cuttings, stuck into an album along with other pictures of him as a baby and a clipping from *The Times* announcing his adoption. He said, "Well, it doesn't look much like me now. No one could tell it was me."

"Anyone can find out," Willy said. "They keep old newspapers filed away in the library."

Alex felt giddy. The printed words danced up and down. He said, "How much is a fortune?"

"A lot of money. I don't know. My Mum says if the house wasn't mortgaged, then it must be worth over a hundred thousand."

"Pounds?"

They looked at each other. Alex blinked shyly. "I don't believe it."

Willy made a fist and punched him lightly. He said, "Lucky swine."

"I don't feel very lucky."

"Why not?"

"It feels funny. Sort of scary. That man, Mr. Fowles, being angry." He looked at the paper. "What does *pressurize* mean?"

"Making someone do something."

Alex said, "My Gran used to take me to see Mrs. Angel. She didn't make me go, not exactly, but I couldn't say no. It felt mean."

"There's an old lady down our street. She can't get out because of her legs. My Mum keeps an eye on her, makes me do her shopping Saturday mornings. It's not much to ask, my Mum says, if I try to get out of it. That's the same sort of thing." Willy punched Alex again, snorting. "Not that we're after her money; she hasn't got any. Only her pension."

Alex said, "My Gran wasn't after her money either. She liked Mrs. Angel. She said so."

Willy said thoughtfully, "I wonder how it got in the papers."

"Someone told them. Laura's friend, Carla, her Dad's a reporter. He lives down the road."

Alex felt his ears singing. Laura had told Carla and she'd told her Dad . . .

He said, "Oh, my Mum will go mad when she sees the paper."

"What for? It's not as if you'd been had up by the police. Stealing or something."

"I don't think she'd mind that so much," Alex said gloomily.

Willy whistled. "She potty or something?"

"No. She just likes things to be fair. If I get all this money . . ." He remembered his Finding Day and the check his grandmother had sent him. That had been only ten pounds more than she'd given Laura, and his mother had been cross about that! A hundred thousand pounds was *ten thousand* times worse! His heart sank—he felt it, like a lead ball dropping down from his chest to his stomach. He wondered if his mother had seen the newspaper. They only had morning papers delivered but Dad often bought an evening paper on the way home from work. Perhaps he would leave it in his raincoat pocket. Alex saw the raincoat in his mind's eye, hanging on a hook in the hall with the rolled-up newspaper sticking out. If he could take it and burn it, Mum wouldn't see it. He said, "I better go home."

As he walked with Willy across the cropped grass, smelling summery sweet from the mowing, his legs felt stumpy and slow. Willy, hopping, pretending to be a one-legged cripple to keep down to Alex's pace, said, "D'you think they'll let you spend some of it? Or will they make you put it all in the bank?"

"Don't know," Alex said. He didn't want to talk about it. But Willy was so excited, it seemed mean, somehow, to be silent and grumpy. Willy's father was out of work and Willy had free school dinners, so his family must be quite poor. Perhaps, Alex thought, his mother and father would let him give some of the money to Willy. He could give all the money away, share it between his parents and Laura and Bob and Ellie. He could send some to Oxfam to help starving children. He felt lighter suddenly and started to run, eager to get home and explain this good plan to his mother, only stopping when he got to the drive to look out for traffic and shout back to Willy, "See you tomorrow."

His mother was in the hall, talking on the telephone. She was saying, "No. That's final. We are making no statement to the press. Absolutely no comment."

She banged the receiver down. She said, "That's the sixth so far. George, can't we stop them?"

Alex's father came out of the living room. He had the newspaper in his hand, folded so that Alex could see the picture and the heavy, black headline. He said, heartily, "Oh, there you are, Alex." And to Alex's mother, "Leave the receiver off, darling."

"That won't stop them. They'll come to the house." Her eyes snapped at Alex. "Where have you been?"

"With Willy." Alex drew in his breath. "He showed me the paper. I didn't know it was so much money. I thought it was only just enough for a bicycle."

"Oh," his mother said. "Oh, you poor baby."

His father put an arm around her shoulders. He said, "Poor seems an odd word to use in the circumstances. Darling, I thought you'd explained to him."

"I tried to. But it's not an easy thing to explain to a child that everything's changed, that he's set apart from his brothers and sisters."

She began to cry. The tears made shiny tracks on her cheeks. Alex's father took out his handkerchief and gave it to her. "Hush, love," he said. "It's not as bad as that. It's not bad at all, really. You're making too much of it." He smiled at Alex to comfort him too. He said, "A mountain out of a molehill."

Alex said, "What does she mean about everything changing?"

"Nothing," his father said. "She's upset . . ."

Alex said, "Willy says it must be more than a hundred thousand pounds. That's what a house costs, Willy says."

His mother stared at him over the handkerchief. Her eyes were still brimming. "You've been talking to *Willy*?"

"I told you, he showed me the newspaper," Alex said patiently. "He knew all about it."

His mother put her head on his father's shoulder and groaned. "Oh, there'll be no peace now, everyone knowing. Oh, I can't *bear* it. We were so happy, a happy family, now everything will be spoiled. It's my mother's fault; she wanted to spoil it. She's always made trouble."

"Rubbish," Alex's father said.

"It's not rubbish. Why do you think she made the poor old woman give Alex that picture? So he should look at it, and wonder . . ."

"That's enough!" Alex's father said loudly. He took her arms and shook her, quite roughly. Then he pushed her into the sitting room. "Sit down," he said. "I'll come in a minute." He closed the door and looked down at Alex. "She doesn't mean half she says."

Alex said, "If she means a quarter, that's quite a lot. I'm sorry, Dad. I don't want the horrible money."

"Look," his father said. "Listen. What money there is, how much, or how little, will go into a trust for you when you're older. Until then, it doesn't concern you. The best thing you can do is forget all about it."

"Mum won't forget."

"Yes she will. She's just in one of her states. She'll get out of it."

Alex sighed. His father took his chin in his hands and looked into his eyes. "As for the rest of it," he said, "you're our boy, nothing can change that. If anything bothers you, come and tell me. Right?"

"Right, Dad," Alex said.

"Nothing you want to ask now?"

"No, Dad."

His father's eyes searched his face with a doubtful expression. Alex felt his eyes flicker. Then his father said, "Good boy. It'll be all right, I promise. Don't worry."

Alex went slowly upstairs. His room had been tidied and cleaned by the lady who came twice a week. She had stood the picture of Mrs. Angel's daughter on the chest of drawers. Alex looked at it and the dark eyes met his. He moved—and they seemed to follow him. Alex knew this was only because she had been looking straight at the camera when the picture was taken, but it made him uncomfortable. He said, under his breath, "Don't watch me. I don't want you to watch me." He opened a drawer and put the photograph away, on its face, at the bottom, and went to find Laura.

Chapter Eight

Laura said, "She could be your proper mother. That's what Mum thinks Gran was hinting at. Course, it's not true. I mean, Gran didn't really believe it. She was just making up a nice story. Mum knows that, really."

"Why is she cross then?"

"You know why! Gran putting ideas in your head. Mischief making. Putting ideas in Mrs. Angel's head, too. Don't you *see*?"

He shrugged, his face stubborn. "Don't want to see," Laura scolded. "Oh, you are boring. If it was me I'd be *glad*, these exciting things happening."

"I wish it was you, then it wouldn't be me," Alex said. "I don't want things to happen. I want them to stay the same. Mum was crying. She's angry with me."

"No, she's not; she's just angry."

"If I wasn't here she wouldn't be, so it's still my fault, isn't it?" Alex stood by the window in Laura's room, fiddling with the window shade. He jerked the tassel and the shade flew up with a snap, breaking the cord. He said, "I wish I could run away."

"I often wish that," Laura said. "Everyone does."

He was looking so utterly miserable that she wanted to shake him. She said, putting her head on one side and pretending to think very deeply, "Suppose it was true!"

"You just said it wasn't."

Laura ignored the pleading in his voice. "I know I said that, but I don't *know*, do I? I mean, you must have had a mother or you wouldn't be here, and she might be still alive, mightn't she? If I was you, I'd be *interested* . . ."

"You're not me," Alex said. "I don't want . . ."

Laura said sternly, "And if I was her, I'd be sorry to think you didn't want to know who I was."

"You're not her," Alex said. Blood darkened his face.

"I said, *if* I was! I know if *I'd* had a little baby and couldn't look after him, I'd like to think he thought of me sometimes. If I knew that he didn't care, I'd be dreadfully sad."

"Shut up."

Laura heard his voice. She saw his face. But she was enjoying herself too much to stop. "I know that if I'd been adopted, even though I loved my Mum and Dad, I'd want to know about my real parents. And if I had some kind of *clue* like you've got, I'd want to *investigate*. I wouldn't just sit about moaning."

"Please," he said. "Please. Don't go on, Laura."

She stopped then, not because he had asked her to, but because she couldn't think how to go on. And once she had stopped, she was alarmed by how scared he looked, his eyes huge and quite black with fear. She said, "It's all right. I was joking. J-O-K-E."

He stammered, "You're as b-bad as G-Gran, making up stories. Only she's not like you, she's not *spiteful*."

If he hadn't said that, if he had been pathetic and cried, she would have apologized. Instead she tossed her head and said, "If that's what you think, I don't care! I suppose you'll go running to Mum and Dad now, poor little boy, complaining about your spiteful big sister."

"No, I won't. But I hate you."

He spoke very quietly and sadly as if he truly meant this. She said, shaken, "So what? You don't have to love me, you're not my real brother. Why don't you run away if you want to, and leave us alone?"

He gave her one blazing glance and ran from the room. She called after him, "Don't be silly. I didn't mean it." But his door had slammed. She went to the landing and stood listening outside his closed door, hoping to hear him crying. But there was no sound and that made her ashamed, and a little scared too. Although Alex never told tales, at least not intentionally, he might this time. Still she did not dare to open his door. She said in a loud voice, "Alex, do you want to go out before supper? If you like, you can borrow

my bike. I shan't be using it. I've got all this homework."

And when he didn't answer, it seemed that there
was nothing more she could do.

She tried to make it up to him. At supper she
smiled and winked and afterward let him switch television programs without once complaining. He didn't
smile or wink back but he didn't scowl either, and
after he had watched a boring half hour about com-
puters, he switched to *Dallas* without being asked.

Laura said, "There's a nature program on.
Wouldn't you rather see that? I don't mind about *Dallas*, not really."

But he shook his head, still unsmiling, still solemn.

He kept out of her way for the rest of that evening
and the next and the next. He went out on his roller
boots while the light lasted; played with Bob and Ellie;
helped their mother get supper and wash up the
dishes. When Laura spoke to him he answered politely, as if they were strangers. If she had not felt so
bad, sick inside about the things she had said to him,
she would have been angry with him for punishing
her. As it was, she longed to be friends again.

Friday afternoon she waited for him at the school
gate. She guessed that the other children were making
fun of him. She had seen him several times in the
playground, surrounded by a giggling group, pink-
faced and desperate. When he came, running ahead
of the rest of his class, head down, bolting past her,

she ran after him. She caught him up and he slowed down beside her. She said, "Are they all being horrible?"

He glanced at her timidly. "Not really. I mean, not unkind. Just teasing. It makes me feel silly."

"They'll get bored soon. Did Willy tell them?"

"I don't know."

"It was rotten of him if he did."

"I didn't ask him not to."

She said indignantly, "There ought to be a law about putting things like that in the papers. It's private. Perhaps you ought to stay home until it's blown over. If Mum knew—"

"Don't tell Mum."

"She ought to know if they're teasing you."

"No. Please. She'd be angry."

"Not angry," Laura said thoughtfully. "I think she's more *scared*." She looked at him slyly, wondering if she dare tell him the idea that had come to her. She knew that she shouldn't. But she couldn't bear not to. She said, "I think she's scared about the bits in the papers in case someone sees them, someone from your real family, and comes to take you away."

"No one came before, did they?" he said, speaking with confidence, as if he had already thought of this possibility and settled it in his mind. "I mean, it was all in the papers then. About me, and my Finding."

"It's different now. You've got all this money. They might be poor people."

He stood still. He stared at her. He said, in a husky

whimper, "Dad wouldn't let them take me away. I wouldn't go. I'd *kill* myself."

"Don't be a ninny. Don't you see, it's exciting! I think you're just feeble!" But she saw that he really was terrified. She said, "It's all right, don't panic. Dad won't let anything happen to hurt you. If someone comes when he isn't there, you could always hide. There's a good place in the loft at the back of the water tank, you could hide there. I'd help you. I wouldn't tell anyone. . . ." She thought of stories she'd read, about wars, about people hiding refugees in attics and cellars. Her mind seemed to take wings and fly. She whispered, "I wouldn't tell, even if I was tortured."

He said nothing. His face had gone tight and scarlet. At last he blurted out miserably, "You said I wasn't your brother."

"You know I didn't mean that. It's not fair, bringing it up."

"You said it though."

"Oh, all right. I'm sorry. *I'm sorry.*"

"No, you're not."

"Yes, I am." And, suddenly, she was. She took his hand and held it tight. "I really am sorry. I'm sorry for everything."

He gave her a funny half smile. He said, "I wish you could turn things back." But his hand stayed in hers as they walked home and she thought he was comforted, not afraid any longer, until they saw the man waiting outside the house. She felt his fingers tug, pulling her back, and heard the fear still in his voice as he said, "Laura, quick, let's go in the side way. Mum said I mustn't . . ."

But they were too late. The man was advancing, smiling kindly and broadly. "Hallo," he said. "Are you Alexander?"

"What do you want?" Laura said, and he smiled at her too.

"Just a picture, young lady. You don't mind that, do you?"

He was holding a camera against his chest. There was a *click*. Then another. He sank to one knee. "Fine," he said, clicking away. "Perfect. Just a couple more. I won't keep you. Look at the camera, sonny; yes, that's right, that's super, a bit of a smile if you can manage it. And again. Good. A nice, happy one there. Thank you both very much."

He stood up, letting the camera dangle from the strap around his neck while he felt in his pocket. "There," he said. "That wasn't too painful, was it? Not like the dentist. What about an ice, or whatever you fancy." He was holding his hand out.

"No, thank you," Laura said. She had been fixed with astonishment. Now she turned her back, shoving Alex ahead of her, keeping him tight against the front door as she thumped the knocker and shouted, "Mum! Open up! *Quick.*"

"She's out. I'm waiting in for the little ones," Gran said as she opened the door. She was munching. She swallowed and brushed biscuit crumbs from her mouth, rather guiltily. "Shouldn't pick between meals," she said. "Bad example. What's wrong, chicken?"

"*Him.*" Laura jerked her head toward the man. "Taking pictures."

The photographer beamed at her grandmother. "Local paper, ma'am. Just one or two shots of this famous young man. Some of the family too, if that's possible. If you'd like to stand by your son, it won't take a minute."

"He's not my son." Gran stood very straight, patting the frills down the front of her blouse. "I don't suppose you want his old grandmother."

"Why not?" the man said. "Though no one would believe it. You look much too young."

Gran smiled happily. Her hands went up to her hair, fluffing it forward. "Do I look all right, Laura?"

"Gran, you mustn't." Laura grabbed her arm and hissed in her ear. "Mum will be furious."

"I could let you have some glossy prints," the man said. "Nice for framing. I'm sure that your daughter—or is it your daughter-in-law?—would be pleased with them."

"No she wouldn't," Laura said.

The photographer looked at her, then at her grandmother. He raised an eyebrow inquiringly.

"I'm afraid she's right," Gran said. "I'm so sorry."

She smiled at him sweetly and shut the door. As she walked down the hall to the kitchen she said, "I can't see it would have done much harm, Laura. I'd have liked a nice picture of Alex and me. Still, you seem to think you know best."

"Mum would have murdered you," Laura said.

"I think that's a little unlikely. Though I admit she's quick-tempered."

"You know what I mean! She'd have gone up in *smoke*!"

Alex laughed at the thought of his mother rising up in a puff of white, like a genie out of a bottle, and Laura turned on him. "It was bad enough letting him take a picture of you. It'll be in the paper. Why on earth did you *smile*?"

"He asked me to."

"Do you always do what people ask?"

"There wasn't time," Alex said. "I didn't think."

Laura raised her eyes to the ceiling. Her grandmother said, "Don't worry, chick. If I'd known he was lurking outside I'd have sent him packing. But I can't really see that it matters so much."

"It does matter," Laura said. "Everyone will know now, not just a few kids at school." She looked fiercely at Alex. "Everyone will know where you live, what you look like. Standing outside our house, grinning!" He was gazing at her, his mouth open. His blank stare infuriated her. "Pleased with yourself, cock-a-hoop; that's what Mr. Fowles said, remember? If he sees you smirking away like that in the paper, he'll come around here, shouting . . ."

Her grandmother saw Alex turn white. She said, "Don't bully, Laura. You're old enough to know better. As for Eric Fowles, I've already given him a good piece of my mind, and if he comes here making trouble, your father will deal with him."

Alex said, in a small, breathy voice, "Suppose he comes when Dad isn't here?"

Gran didn't hear him. She had turned to the sink to fill up the kettle. She said, "The man's a fool. He can shout as much as he likes, but it won't get him anywhere. He's put himself in the wrong, anyway, walking off with poor Angel's bits and pieces that he'd no right to. Your mother's gone to the lawyer to sort that out now, and I think you'll find he'll get his comeuppance." She put the kettle on the stove and smiled brightly at Laura. "So let's have no more silliness, chicken. It's just jealousy, I suppose; that's only natural, but you must try not to take it out on poor Alex."

"I'm not jealous," Laura said, growling like thunder.

Her grandmother pursed her lips. "Then why make all this fuss and old taradiddle? You're as bad as your mother. I really don't know what she's on about half the time. Except that it's all my fault, apparently."

"Well, it is, isn't it? You took Alex to see Mrs. Angel, making him suck up to her, making up *lies*, pretending he might be her *grandson*—"

"I did no such thing. You watch your tongue, miss!"

Laura said, "I don't mean you said it straight out. Only hinted."

"You're too young to understand," her grandmother said. She made the tea, warming the pot, measuring out the tea leaves, pouring on boiling water, concentrating on this simple task to avoid looking at Laura.

"*I'm not too young!*" Laura shouted. "That's what grown-ups always say. As if being young makes you blind and deaf too. I *heard* you, I heard you and Mum. If it wasn't for you Mrs. Angel would never have left any money to Alex. So it's your fault, making everything horrible, all the trouble is your fault. . . ."

"It isn't. It's mine," Alex said. "If I wasn't here, if I'd never been *found*, everyone would be happy."

They saw his face, shocked and pale. Then he ran from the room. They looked at each other. "I forgot he was here," Laura said. All her anger had left her.

Her grandmother sighed. "Go after him, chick. We don't want your mother to come back and find him upset."

She was more worried about that than she was about Alex, Laura thought. But she didn't say so. Gran was looking so weary suddenly, sitting down at the table, her shoulders hunched, her face crumpled. "He'll be all right," Laura said. "Have a nice cup of tea. It'll make you feel better."

She went slowly upstairs. Guilt made her reluctant. What could she say to him? She thought—*Give him time to cool off.*

She stood at the landing window. She could see Bob and Ellie and the three kids from next door on the far side of the Fields. They were playing What's the Time, Mr. Wolf. Bob was the Wolf; the others were creeping up behind his turned back. Ellie was almost upon him and, watching her, Laura knew what she was feeling, remembering herself playing this game when she had been little, sneaking slowly forward, step by step, excited and fearful. When Bob whirled around suddenly, Laura felt her own stomach lurch as if, by some magic, she was inside Ellie's skin, running on shaky legs, the Wolf chasing after her. Then she saw Ellie fall flat on her face and lie still. She didn't move, even when Bob bent over her and tried to lift her. He crouched down; the other children stood around. *Fooling*, Laura thought. All the same, she was frightened. She flew down the stairs and out of the house, her heart pounding.

Ellie wasn't hurt. By the time Laura reached her, she was bored with pretending. When Laura knelt beside her, she rolled over, scarlet and sulky. "They won't let me be Wolf," she complained. "It's not fair."

"She doesn't play properly," Bob said. "She doesn't wait long enough, she's just silly."

Ellie scrambled up and flew at him. Laura caught hold of her, laughing. "If you don't give her a turn, she'll never learn, will she? Come on, Ellie. I'll be Wolf with you and show you."

She played with them, teaching Ellie to count at least up to twelve before she turned to shout "Dinner time," and then went on playing for the fun of it, slipping back into being small again—five or six, feeling happy and free. She forgot about Alex, or half forgot, pushing him to the back of her mind, until she saw Bob standing still, staring. She looked where he was looking and saw Mr. Fowles on the edge of the Field. "That man's watching us," Bob said. "He's been watching us all the time. I don't like him."

"Don't watch him back," Laura said. "Just don't pay any attention."

Alarm rang in her mind. She wondered if Alex had looked out of his window and seen him. And at once she knew she shouldn't have left him. She said to Bob, "I've got to go. It's time you came home too. Bring Ellie with you," and ran back to the house as if a real wolf, sharp fangs and snapping jaws, ran behind her.

Chapter Nine

Everyone had always loved Alex. He was used to being loved. He had never worried, as Laura did, about the horrible things people might say about him behind his back.

Now, suddenly, it seemed he was surrounded by enemies. Laura was jealous of him; his grandmother had said so. His mother was angry. Even if she wasn't angry with him, she was angry because of him, and she had quarreled with his grandmother about him. And Mr. Fowles, standing on the edge of the Field, watchful and menacing, hated him. He might come to the house and do something dreadful. Worse than that, his real mother and father might come. Since everyone was so angry, Mum and Dad might let them take him away.

He packed his school bag with a clean pair of socks, his Adidas running shoes, a thick jersey, his solar calculator, and his Post Office savings book that had twenty-seven pounds in it. He had one pound and sixty-five pence in cash in his pocket. He left his front door key on the chest where Laura would find it and slipped out of the house the back way, through the gate at the end of the garden, and into the narrow alley where the dustbins were kept.

No one saw him go. He went by the back streets, avoiding the Fields, and saw no one he knew. When he reached the main road, he caught the first bus that stopped and sat in the front, behind the driver's cab, and kept his head down.

The bus took him to the City. He got off the bus and walked with the crowd on the pavements. Everyone seemed busy and purposeful, hurrying home at the end of the day. The thought of them all going home made him feel lonely and miserable. Hungry, too. He bought a hot dog full of spicy sausage and mustard, and felt better, although the mustard had made his mouth dry.

Thirsty, he wandered through a maze of little lanes, past public houses that were so full this warm evening that people were spilling out onto the pavements. He wished he could buy a bottle of lemonade or ask for a glass of water, but it was against the law for children to go into pubs, and someone might ask him what he was doing, a boy on his own in the city.

He walked on, turning corners at random, until he came to a small cemetery at the side of a church. It looked quiet and peaceful and he decided to rest for a little and plan what to do. There was a tramp sleeping on one of the tombstones, his old coat pulled over his head. Alex settled on another stone at a discreet distance, watching the tramp turning and muttering in his sleep, and wondered if it was against the law to sleep in a churchyard. The stone was surprisingly comfortable, but he was still thirsty and beginning to be hungry again. He looked at his watch and saw that it was nearly nine o'clock. At home they would have had supper by now. Perhaps they thought he had gone out for the evening, gone to see Willy. Although he always told Mum when he was going out, she hadn't been there to tell. She might think that he had told Gran, and that Gran had forgotten. If Laura hadn't found his front door key, there was no reason why they should worry. Perhaps they didn't care anyway. Perhaps they were all sitting around the big kitchen table, happy, and laughing. Happy without him. Happy because he wasn't there, making trouble.

A lump came into his throat and his eyes smarted. "Well, that's why you ran away, wasn't it, so you wouldn't be such a horrible nuisance to everyone?" he said in a cross, scolding voice, and this made him feel worse. Of course he was a horrible nuisance, a horrible person! They must all be glad to be rid of him! As Laura had said, he wasn't one of the family. Even if she hadn't meant it altogether, she must have meant it with part of her mind or she wouldn't have said it. Oh, she had *pretended* to like him, but she couldn't, really, or she would have stopped him from running away. He'd waited and waited in his room and then he'd looked out of the window and seen her playing with Bob and Ellie, running and laughing, not caring about him at all. She wasn't his friend; she was a traitor. She'd promised to hide him, but that was how traitors behaved. They said they were on your side, made you trust them, then they gave you away.

A painful sob shook him. He choked it back and knuckled his fists in his eyes. A voice said, above him, "You all right, sonny?"

Alex looked up at a bearded face under a helmet. The policeman said, "Not lost or anything, are you?"

Alex shook his head. He couldn't speak. The word "lost" seemed to close up his throat.

"Time you were at home, isn't it? Little chap like you?"

Alex found his voice then. "I'm not little. I'm eleven. I'm just a bit small for my age."

"All the same. Not a healthy place to be hanging about this time of night." He glanced at the sleeping tramp and smiled kindly at Alex. "Unsuitable company. What are you up to?"

"Just sitting," Alex said. "Thinking." He added, boldly, "No law against thinking, is there?"

"Not that I know of." The policeman hesitated, then said, quite sharply, "Where do you live?"

"Finsbury Fields."

"How are you getting home?"

"Number Four bus."

"Got the fare?"

Alex pulled some coins out of his pocket and displayed them on his palm. A sudden hope seized him. Perhaps the policeman would rescue him, call up a police car on his walkie-talkie and send him home in it. But he only glanced at the money and said, "Okay, get going. I should look sharpish, too. There's rain coming by the looks of it. Don't want your Mum to be worried, do we?"

He gave Alex a keen, level look, as if some doubt still remained. Alex thought—*If I cry, he'll do something.* But he was too proud. He said, "No, I'll go straight home now. Thank you."

He did his best to smile. But as he walked away, without looking back, he felt lonely and fearful. Telling lies always made him uncomfortable; if they found out he had lied to a policeman, they might put him in prison! Laura would say that was nonsense, he knew, but she wasn't here. If she were, she would know what to do now, make a good plan, decide where to go. He thought—*Laura would make it exciting!*

He squared his shoulders and marched on. He would have to manage without her. She was always bossing him about anyway. Bossy, as well as a traitor! He could look after himself. People in books were always running away, so it couldn't be all that difficult. He wasn't far from the river. He could sleep in one of the gardens on the Embankment, or if it did rain—and the sky was beginning to look a menacing purple—he could find shelter. The City was empty at night. He could sleep in a doorway and go to a Post Office tomorrow morning and get out his money. Twenty-seven pounds would last quite a long time. He could take a train and go into the country and find a forest to live in, like Robin Hood. He could buy food in tins and store them in a hollow tree while he taught himself to catch rabbits. He could find out how to do that if he went to a library, and he could look up other things, like which berries and mushrooms were safe to eat. . . .

Thinking of food made saliva come into his mouth. It was beginning to rain now, not much, only spitting, but it made the air colder. He turned into a narrow street and saw people sitting at tables under an awning outside a coffee shop. He went into the shop, bought a bottle of orange soda and a cheese and tomato sandwich, and sat down at one of the tables. A plump lady with a cheerful, round face shifted her chair to give him more room. She smiled at him and he smiled back as he bit into his sandwich. He ate slowly, to make it last. The lady said, in a friendly voice, "That's not much of a meal for a growing boy. Have a piece of fruit pie. Go on, old Poll will treat you." He shook his head but she got up, groaning a bit as if heaving her heavy body off her chair was an effort, went into the shop, and came out with a huge wedge of pie. She said, "There, get stuck into that. Don't thank me, my pleasure. I don't like to see kids going hungry."

The pie crust was thick and dry and the fruit, a soggy mixture of apples and blackberries, so sour that it made his mouth tingle. He persevered because the kind lady was watching him. She wore a shabby coat, pinned together in front with a big safety pin, and he had noticed when she had gone into the shop that she was wearing canvas shoes with holes in the toes on her bare feet. He thought she must be very poor, so it had been generous of her to buy him the pie. "It's very nice," he said. "Thank you."

He saw the boys out of the corner of his eye. A group of them, five or six, giggling. One of them was carrying a bucket. He didn't see what they did, only heard their excited laughter as they raced away, and then a shriek from the next table. A girl jumped up, slapping at her neck. "Something *hit* me, something horrible! *Ugh!* What is it?"

The man with her laughed. He was crouching under the table; he stood up, his hands cupped together. "Here," he said, "only a baby frog; that couldn't hurt you."

Alex went to look. The tiny creature was trying to crawl up the man's fingers. "It's a toad," Alex said. "Frogs hop."

"This one fell from the sky," the man said. "Hey, there's one by your foot. Talk of raining cats and dogs, it's frogs today. Or toads, if you say so." He dropped the toad he was holding beside the other one and pushed them both off the curb with his foot. The rain was heavier now, drumming on the awning and running fast in the gutter, and the baby toads swirled along in the water toward the storm drain.

"They'll drown," Alex said, too late to save the first toad but catching the second before it fell through the grating. It scrabbled against his palm, tickling him pleasantly.

"What are you going to do with it, laddie?" The fat woman was watching him with amusement. "Take it 'ome for a pet?"

"Toads are getting quite rare," Alex said. "I read

about that in the newspaper. I'll put it in the grass in the garden on the Embankment. It'll be nice and wet there and no one will tread on it." He hoped she wouldn't notice that he hadn't finished his pie. He said, "I'd better go quickly, or it'll get too hot in my hand."

He wondered if the little toads had really rained down from the sky. Perhaps a bird had picked them up from the pond where they lived and flown with them over the City and dropped them. "Poor little toad, far from home," he said, stroking its cool, dry head tenderly. "You must be so lonely."

He had forgotten about the boys. He came upon them as he turned the corner at the bottom of the street. One of them was smoking and flicking ash into the bucket that he was holding, and the others were standing around, sniggering. The smoker saw Alex. He said, "They got a fright back there, didn't they? Bet they didn't know what had happened."

Alex looked into the bucket, which was full of small toads, a heaving, struggling, dark mass. "You shouldn't throw them about," he said. "You might hurt them."

"Aw, come off it," a boy said. "Just a bit of fun, ain't it?"

Alex grinned. It *had* been funny: the silly girl screaming, toads appearing from nowhere. He said, "Where did you get them?"

"From the canal. There's toads all over the banks. Just hatched out of tadpoles."

"Are you going to put them back?" Alex showed them his toad, quiet now in his hand. "I was going to put mine in the garden. But a canal would be better."

One boy laughed. The smoker said, "Maybe we will at that. Pop it in the bucket with its brothers and sisters." Alex hesitated. The way they were watching him made him vaguely uneasy. But the boy with the cigarette smiled encouragingly and he dropped his toad in with the others. At once, they all started to laugh. The smoker drew on his cigarette, flaming the tip red, and made as if to stub it out in the bucket. Alex shouted, *"No!"* and the boy laughed louder, running backward, holding the bucket high, whirling it around his head. Baby toads flew through the air, landing on heads and necks, wriggling down shirt fronts, crawling away between dancing feet, while the boys roared wild with laughter or, if they had a toad inside their clothes, squealed hysterically.

"Stop it," Alex begged. "Oh, please stop. You'll kill them." He hopped up and down, trying not to tread on the toads on the ground, trying to reach the bucket. Then someone pushed him hard in the back and he fell. He staggered up and they surrounded him, laughing; open mouths like dark caves guarded by white teeth, jeering at him. He said, "It's against the law! Cruelty to animals is against the law. I could call a policeman."

" 'Ark at him," one of them said. "Who does 'e think he is? Super grass?"

Somebody laughed, but it was an uglier sound than

before. Threatening. Alex stood still. They were all much bigger than he was. He said, pleadingly, "It's unkind to hurt animals. If you just let them go, I won't tell a policeman."

"That's brilliant, that's reely fantastic," the smoker said. He spoke in a high, speaky voice, mimicking Alex. "Pick 'em up, taken 'em safely back to their mummies and daddies and he won't fetch the fuzz." He thrust his face close to Alex. "What makes you think we're going to give you the chance, eh? Comin' along, interfering. Who *asked* you, that's what I'd like to know."

"I didn't mean to interfere," Alex said. He thought that a lot of toads had probably made their escape by now. He said, "Please let me go."

"Oh, so it's please let *me* go now, is it? Never mind the poor little froggies. Goin' to make it worth our while, are you?"

"Leave him be," someone said. Alex couldn't tell who had spoken. Another boy had opened his school bag, which he had dropped when he was knocked over, and was peering inside. He held up Alex's Post Office savings book, and then shook out the rest of the things on the ground. They all gathered around. One boy picked up the calculator. "Please," Alex said, "that's new. It's a present."

"I'll give you a present." The smoker lifted the bucket and emptied it over Alex's head. The last toads showered over him, slithering down his face like small, cold, rubbery balls. One slipped under the neck of his shirt. He grabbed it and threw it away, shivering with a sudden, sickening disgust. He was trying hard not to cry.

Above the screams of laughter, he could hear shouting. The fat lady from the coffee shop seized a boy by his shoulder, spun him around to face her, and gave him a clout that sent him reeling. "Anyone else want one?" she asked, glaring around her. "No, didn't think you would. Clear off the lot of you, clear off home. If you've got homes to go to."

She turned to Alex. "Blimey," she said, "what a sight. Here, let me get at you."

Her red face beamed down like a friendly sun. She brushed toads off his chest, off his forehead, picked several out of his hair. Then she took a piece of tissue out of her pocket and spat on it lavishly. She said, while she scrubbed him, "Well, I never did! Lucky I heard them. Though they were making enough noise, all that yellin' and bawlin'. Didn't mean much harm, I expect, just young hooligans out on the razzle. Not enough between the ears, that's the trouble. How'd you get mixed up with them, nice boy like you?"

They had all disappeared. Beyond the street lamps, darkness gleamed in the rain. The empty bucket lay on its side and only a few toads were still visible, crawling on the pavement and in the gutter. Alex's bag was there, but it was empty. His running shoes, his sweater, and his clean socks, rolled in a neat ball, lay beside it. Alex said, "They've stolen my savings book and my calculator."

"Never mind, lovey, you're not hurt, that's the main thing."

"They hurt the poor toads."

"Don't worry about them, my lovey. They'll find a safe place. Nature's clever that way." She gave a final dab at his face and stood back to look at him. "There, you look tidy now. Pick your things up. I'm not much good at stooping, too thick 'round the middle. That's right, fasten the straps up, now you're sorted out nicely. Lucky old Poll came by. I expect those rascals have made themselves scarce, but perhaps you'd better come to the station with me just in case."

She walked faster than might have been expected for a woman of her heavy build; so fast that Alex had to trot to keep up with her. Glancing sideways, he wondered how old she was. Her frizzy hair was mostly gray, but there were orange streaks in it. The skin of her face was unwrinkled, tight over her bones and smooth as a balloon full of air. Older than his mother, he thought, younger than his grandmother. He said, "Do you have any children?"

"Bless you, no! Though I suppose I do in a manner of speaking. No kids of my own, is the answer. But that reminds me, I've got to call in at the market."

"Aren't the shops closed now?"

"Not where I live. They stay open all hours." They had reached the Tube station. He followed her to the machines and stood beside her while she took coins from her pocket. She said, "Where d'you want to go, laddie?"

"I don't know."

She looked at him. He said, very fast, "Can I come home with you? Just for the night. I won't be a nuisance."

As soon as he'd spoken he knew it was foolish. She would want to know where he lived, why he wasn't at home this time of night; she might even ask for his telephone number and ring his mother and father. He waited for this to happen, a mixture of hope and fear churning inside him. But, to his amazement, she simply put another coin into the ticket machine. She said, "I daresay there's room for a little one. And I could do with a spare pair of hands with my shopping."

Chapter Ten

Alex was so tired that he fell asleep in the train, his head on Poll's comfortable shoulder. When she woke him, and he stumbled up and followed her onto the platform and up the stairs to the street, he was too sleepy to notice the name of the station. Out in the noisy main road, with trucks crashing past throwing up dirty spray from the puddles, he realized that he had no idea where he was, in what part of London. He wanted to ask her, but she was forging ahead so fast, holding his hand and dragging him after her, that he had no breath to speak with. Most of the shops that they passed were closed, with dark entrances and shutters over the windows, but the supermarket was a blaze of light, loud with taped music, and busy with people.

Poll gave him a trolley. "Follow me along," she said. "That's the quickest way."

She threw in several bags of potatoes, three cauliflowers, apples, bananas, and so many loaves of bread that he didn't bother to count them. She must have a lot of people to feed, he thought, and wondered who they could be if she didn't have any children. She stopped at the meat counter, looked around briefly, and said, "Quite a load in that trolley. Got some room in that bag of yours, have you?"

His school bag was slung around his shoulder. She unfastened the straps, turned back the flap, and put a leg of lamb, a jumbo pack of minced beef, and a chicken inside it. She did up the straps again. She winked at him merrily. "There's a good boy. Just keep right behind me."

There was no line at the checkout. Poll plonked the things from the trolley in a pile on the counter. A pretty Indian girl rang them up. Alex put his bag on the counter and nudged Poll to remind her, but she paid no attention. The girl smiled at him. She said, "You look a tired little boy," and gave him a bar of nut and raisin chocolate from a stand next to the till. She said, in a sweet, lilting voice, "I think your mummie forgot you."

Alex felt his ears singing. Out in the street, Poll took the bag from him. "Too heavy for you," she said, and slung it on her own shoulder.

Alex clutched the sleeve of her coat. He stammered, "B-but you didn't . . . I m-mean, we forgot . . ."

She didn't look at him. She said, "I've got those great boys to think of. Can't feed them on taters and scraps. Got to keep their strength up."

She was charging ahead again, sturdy legs moving like pistons. Following her, Alex peeped nervously back over his shoulder, afraid that someone—the girl from the checkout, a policeman—would come shouting after them. He had carried the bag out of the shop, he had *stolen.* . . . That was worse than telling lies to a policeman. He was an outlaw now, as well as a runaway.

Bemused, heavyhearted, he caught up with Poll. She gave him a quick smile. "Not much farther now, lovey."

They crossed the road. Poll didn't stop to look; she just put up a hand and a truck stopped with a loud hiss of brakes. They turned into a dark street where most of the street lamps were broken and some of the houses boarded up, the front gardens full of rubble and rubbish. "Home Sweet Home," Poll said, pushing open a rickety wooden gate and sidling past a big motorbike that took up most of the narrow path. "The times I've told 'im to put it 'round the back in the yard," she grumbled, setting her bags down and hammering on the door.

A light came on in the hall. A chain rattled and the door opened. An enormous man filled the doorway. He said, "Forgot your key again, Poll? Late, ain't you? We're famished, waiting for dinner."

"I've got my key," Poll said. "Just keepin' you on your toes. And dinner's when I say, not before."

The huge man looked down at Alex. "What's this, then? Not our dinner, I hope."

"He helped me get it," Poll said. "So be civil, if you don't mind. Found him down the City. Not a night for a little lad to sleep out, I thought. He can bunk up with Bill."

"That's all right, then," the big man said. From his

immense height, he grinned down at Alex. "Glad you're not our dinner, I must say. Thought the old girl might've fancied a bit of a boy stew."

Though this was meant to be funny, Alex was too tired to smile. Poll had disappeared somewhere. The man said, "Let's go and find Bill then, young kiddo. Meet your sleeping partner. What's your monniker?"

"Alex." He hoped this was the right answer.

"Right then, young Alex. I'm Samson. My old ma was keen on the Bible. Bit of a fool name. Just luck that I grew to fit it."

"How do you do?" Alex said. He was feeling so weary, suddenly, that everything seemed to be dancing around him. Samson said something that he couldn't hear, and then Alex found himself lifted, cradled like a baby against a broad, solid chest. Samson was carrying him down the hall into a hot, brightly lit room with a blazing fire in the hearth and shots and screams from the television. "Turn that down and clear off the sofa, you rank idle lot," Samson said. "We got a visitor."

Soft cushions beneath him, faces looming above him. A black girl wearing a glittering dress, blue and silver; a man with a coxcomb of hair, stiff scarlet spikes sticking up; a skinny boy in a yellow T-shirt that had HERE COMES TROUBLE written in black letters across it. Laura's friend, Carla, had a similar T-shirt; when she turned around it said, HERE GOES TROUBLE. Laura had wanted one like it, but Mum had said no. Why she had said no, Alex couldn't remember. He wondered if the boy in the T-shirt was Bill. He tried to smile at the faces but they swam out of focus, blurred around the edges, and the glaring light stung his eyes. He felt giddy, and sick. It would be dreadful to be sick in this strange house with these strangers watching, messing up their carpets, their sofa . . .

Samson said, "The kid's all in. Anything left in that bottle? Best medicine I know of." Other voices murmured above him. "Better ask Poll first." "Get away; Poll don't know everything. Course it won't hurt 'im." Then a warm arm was under his neck lifting his head, and the black girl, kneeling beside him, was holding a tumbler. She said, "If you're feeling queer this'll settle you." He sipped, felt his mouth burn, and gagged. The girl said, "Come on, treasure, only brandy, drink up for Petal."

A pretty name, he thought. She had a nice voice too, soft and coaxing. He sat up a bit, gulped, and swallowed. The brandy was fire in his throat, but to please her he emptied the glass, and almost at once began to feel better, not sick anymore, only so sleepy that he couldn't keep his eyes open. He tried to open them, fluttering heavy eyelids, but the room was spinning around him again and the sofa was rocking like a boat on the sea. He heard someone say, laughing, "That's a right knockout you gave him, Samson. A skinful."

Then Petal said, close to his ear, "You're all right, treasure. Just let go, off to sleep now."

And because she sounded so comforting and was holding his hand, he slipped into sleep as if rocked in a cradle.

Chapter Eleven

"I knew that he'd run away as soon as I found his front door key," Laura said to her grandmother. "If they'd looked for him straightaway they might have found him. Instead of just saying he must have gone to see Willy, and *waiting*."

Her grandmother was breaking eggs into a bowl. She said, without looking up, "If you were so sure, why didn't you say?"

"I did, when they started to worry—Dad ringing the police and Mum saying he must have had some dreadful accident. Then I thought, if he'd just gone out, he'd have taken his key. That's what I meant when I said that I *knew*. I mean, once I thought about it, I wasn't surprised. It was as if I'd known all along, really."

"Oh, we're all wise after the event," her grandmother said—more to herself, it seemed, than to Laura.

"If I'd told them to start with, they wouldn't have believed me."

"That's not what I meant. Don't be silly, dear."

"That's right," Laura said. "That's just what they would have said. *Don't be silly, dear.*" She sniffed righteously.

"Why did he run away?" Major Bumpus said.

It was the first time he had spoken since Laura had burst into her grandmother's kitchen. He had been sitting in the most comfortable chair, quietly listening. Now he fired this question so sharply that Laura felt herself stiffen. But it was only his manner. He was smiling and his eyes were kind. Laura smiled back and said, "You made me jump."

Her grandmother shook her head at him. "Don't you bring your military habits into my kitchen, Monty! Especially if you want me to cook breakfast for you!"

She was scolding him in a laughing way. "Sorry," he said. "Thought she might know, that's all. Seems a bright girl. Fond of young Alex. Nearer his age than we are. Didn't mean to bark at her, Amy."

Though he spoke more gently, his blue gaze watched Laura intently. She shifted from one foot to the other.

Her grandmother was watching her too. She said, "There's been a lot of fuss—about the inheritance."

"Fuss?" Major Bumpus said. "What kind of fuss?"

Laura and her grandmother looked at each other. Both knew more than they wanted to say, Laura thought. She said, reluctantly, "Teasing and things. I teased him a bit."

Her grandmother nodded, and sighed. Then said, quite briskly and brightly, "That's all it was, chicken. Alex took it the wrong way, I expect, but it wasn't your fault."

She was being kind, comforting Laura, and perhaps herself too. But it made Laura feel worse. Gran didn't know half of it! "I was *horrid* to him," she said in a deliberately childish, sad voice, hanging her head.

Major Bumpus said, "Boys have to learn to put up with a bit of teasing. Especially from their sisters. Had three myself, so I know."

Laura's grandmother sighed again. "Alex is a sensitive boy."

Laura scowled. Last night she had felt dreadful, ashamed and afraid. This morning, coming downstairs to find her mother and father pale and swollen eyed after a sleepless night, she had felt, suddenly, very angry with Alex. It was despicable to run away, making their mother cry, frightening everyone, punishing her because she had teased him. That was all she had done, just a bit of sisterly teasing. Major Bumpus was right, boys had to learn to put up with it. Alex was just being feeble, wanting everyone to be nice to him always. *Feeble and spoiled*, she thought, fuming. And now Gran was calling him *sensitive!*

"Stupid," she said. "That's what he is. *Stupid*." A thought came to her, ringing clear in her head. "Running away because of that nasty photographer, because he was scared that Mum would be angry if his picture got in the papers. I mean, that really is *dumb!*"

Her grandmother said, "Laura! Do you really think that was the reason?"

"Why not?" Major Bumpus said. "Out of the mouths of babes and sucklings. Not that Laura here is a baby, of course." He leaned forward in his chair and bobbed his head at her; a quaint, courtly little bow, as an apology. "But perhaps she's hit the nail on the head. He seemed a manly little feller to me. Not the sort to bolt after a few sharp words from his sister. But if he thought he'd upset his *mother*—well, you know, that's a different kettle of fish altogether."

He looked from Laura to her grandmother with a pleased smile. "There," he said. "That's the answer."

"Oh, dear," Laura's grandmother said. "I don't know . . ."

"Take it from me, Amy," Major Bumpus said. "A boy has a very special feeling for his mother. I know that I had a very special feeling for mine. I'd have cut off my right hand rather than hurt her."

Laura saw doubt in her grandmother's face. She said, "Alex *was* scared Mum would be angry. He really *hates* it when she's unhappy."

"Natural," Major Bumpus said. "Boylike."

"If you tell your mother that, Laura," her grandmother said, "I think that I'll never forgive you. Don't you see, Monty? It would be dreadful for her to think that Alex ran away because he was afraid of her."

"Not afraid *of* her, Amy," Major Bumpus said. "Afraid of distressing her."

"It comes to the same thing. Laura, you promise me, won't you?"

Laura stared in amazement. Gran sounded so anxious. She said, "I don't see why you mind so much how Mum feels, when you're always quarreling. And she did keep on about how awful it was, everyone knowing. It'll be worse than ever now, won't it? I mean, there will be more in the papers, now he's gone missing, and Dad said they were going to put his picture on television this evening. On the news. In case someone's seen him."

"Your mother won't mind that kind of publicity," Major Bumpus said. "As much and as soon as possible. Don't want the trail to get cold. Strike while the iron's hot. Though I should think the young shaver will turn up any minute. Boys are fond of their stomachs. Back as soon as he's hungry."

"He can buy food," Laura said. "He's got his Post Office savings book. It's got twenty-seven pounds in it."

"Ah!" Major Bumpus said. "Excellent! The police will get on to the Post Office. He'll be picked up soon as he tries to draw his cash out. So don't you worry, young lady."

"Don't worry your poor mother, either," Gran said. "About that photographer, or anything else you happen to think of. Just tell her that I'll be over in about an hour and take the little ones off her hands for the day. Major Bumpus and I thought we might take them to the Whale Room at the Natural History Museum.

Would you like bacon with your scrambled eggs, Monty?"

"They'd rather see the dinosaurs," Laura said.

"Dinosaurs, whales, we can see the lot," Major Bumpus said heartily. "D'you want to come with them, young lady? More the merrier!"

"It's very kind of you," Laura said. "But my father has gone with the police to help look for Alex and I think *someone* ought to stay with my mother."

She gave her grandmother a withering look. Gadding about, when she ought to stay at home, worrying! *Run across and see Gran, Laura darling*, her mother had said. *She'll be so upset.* But here she was, not weeping and wringing her hands, but dressed in a pretty silk blouse and skirt, her hair neatly curled, cooking bacon and eggs for the Major! A pleasant sizzling came from the stove. Laura said, "Mum couldn't eat any breakfast. I think I'd better go back now and make her some coffee."

She was pleased with this last remark. She hoped it would make her grandmother feel guilty. All the same, she was quite glad that Gran would be out of the way. It made her more important. She would be the only one to look after her mother, hold her hand when she cried, persuade her to eat a piece of toast with her coffee, tell her the comforting things Major Bumpus had said, answer the telephone. A television team was coming early this afternoon, and Mum and Dad were going to send a message to Alex and ask anyone who might have seen him to get in touch with the police. They might even put her on television, Laura thought, and all her friends would be able to watch her. She wondered if Mum would notice if she put on her new jeans and lace blouse. Perhaps she could wash her hair. . . .

It didn't work out quite like that. She had no time to comfort her mother, change her clothes, or wash her hair. When her father came home at midday, Laura was on her knees in the kitchen, sorting out the junk at the bottom of a cupboard while her mother stood on the steps, scrubbing the shelves where the best china was kept.

Dad stood in the doorway. He said, "What on earth are you doing?"

"What does it look like?" Laura said. "Turning out. Tidying. Don't ask me why."

Her mother came down the steps, pushing her hair back. She said, "All that stuff was so filthy. I know we hardly ever use it, but I thought if I took it down and washed it and put it back, that would be a job done."

Dad looked at the dusty dishes piled in the sink, on the draining board, on the table. "It'll take a while, won't it?"

Laura said, "I'll do it, Dad. I don't mind. I wish you'd make her stop. Lie down, or something."

Her mother smiled. "She's been so good, George. I don't know how I could have got through the morning without her. Mother has taken Ellie and Bob. I had to do something. . . ." She caught her breath and let it out in a small, shaky laugh. And then said, casually, as if it was nothing very important, just something she would quite like to know, "Have you found him?"

Dad shook his head and she sat down on a chair. Her neck had gone red in patches and her mouth was fixed in a funny, stretched smile. "Oh, dear," she said. "Oh, dear."

She sounded so helpless and hopeless, it gave Laura a pain in her chest. She took her hand and patted it as she had planned to do before her mother had started on cleaning the cupboards. She said, "It's all right, Mum, really. He'll turn up. Major Bumpus says he'll turn up as soon as he's hungry."

"There was a storm last night," her mother said. "It was *raining*."

"He'll have found somewhere dry to sleep," Laura said. "A bus shelter or something. Alex is sensible."

"Who's Major Bumpus?" Her father sounded bewildered.

"A friend of Gran's. Her boyfriend." Laura giggled; the excitement that had been mounting inside her all morning made her feel weak and silly. "He's gone with Gran to take Bob and Ellie to the Natural History Museum."

"You know, George," her mother said. "I told you my mother had an admirer. Retired from the Army. She picked him up on the Fields."

"Met him," Laura said. "*Picked up* doesn't sound nice. I told him Alex had his Post Office savings book with him. When I found his key, I looked for the book. I guessed that he'd take it. I told you last night, don't you remember? Major Bumpus said if Alex tries to draw out his money, the police will be able to find him."

"The police have got his savings book," her father said. "A boy picked it up and handed it in."

"You mean Alex *lost* it? He wouldn't do that, he's ever so careful."

"I know that," her father said. His expression, the tone of his voice, held a warning. He said, "It was found in the City. Not far from the river."

Laura's mother said, "No! Oh, *no*, George." She stood up and moved toward him, hands held out in front of her like a blind person feeling the way, and he put his arms around her.

"Hush," he said. "Hang on, darling. Alex would never . . ."

He looked at Laura and stopped. For a second she felt cold, as if her veins ran with cold water. Then she said, furious because her father had frightened her, "Oh, you are *morbid*. Of course Alex wouldn't jump in the river! I know what happened! I bet you! Another boy stole the book and got scared and threw it away. Or someone kidnapped Alex, and he dropped the book for a clue. Like you do in a paper chase."

Her father said, "Run along, darling. I'll talk to you later."

Her ears sang with rage. *"Run along, run along?* Why don't you *listen*? Mr. Fowles hates Alex. He stands out there watching. He's been horrible, and Alex was

scared of him coming to get him because of the
money, and he was scared about his real parents too.
But you don't listen to him any more than you listen
to me, and you don't tell him anything, either. You
just let him find out on his own. Serves you right that
he's run away. I wish I'd gone with him, though you
love him more than you love me, so you wouldn't
care, would you?"

They were looking at her, their faces so still that
she couldn't tell what they were thinking. Then her
mother said, "I think we'd better ring the police about
Mr. Fowles, George. Once that's done, perhaps the
three of us can sit down and talk properly."

Chapter Twelve

Alex woke up inside a bright, dancing balloon; shimmering colors like splinters of glass in his eyes. The walls of the small room were covered with Day-Glo posters. As he moved his head they seemed to move too: flash, and change color.

He tried not to look at them. He sat up very cautiously. On the pillow beside him in the narrow bed there was a mane of red spiky hair. Its owner muttered and groaned and tugged the covers up higher.

Alex needed to pee. He slid out of bed. He was still wearing his clothes. And not only his clothes, but his shoes. He wasn't surprised by this; he felt much too ill. When he stood up, his head throbbed, his bones ached. He walked carefully to the door feeling as breakable as an egg; one sharp tap and his head would crack open.

Outside the door was a landing—bare boards and peeling paint—and several doors, all closed. Luckily, the door to the bathroom was open. The bathtub had a grimy ring around it and a lot of dark hairs in the plug hole. The flush didn't work on the lavatory. He pushed it up and down several times. There was a juddering thump in the pipes, but no water came.

He went to the landing and listened. Someone was downstairs; he could hear the television. He looked at his watch, wondering what program was on. It was five o'clock. There was no television at five in the morning. So it must be five in the afternoon. It seemed to take him a long time to work this out. Perhaps he was still asleep, dreaming. He pinched himself and it hurt, so he must be awake. He hadn't had any breakfast or lunch. But he didn't feel hungry.

The television was suddenly louder. A door had opened downstairs and a black girl was looking up at him. His mind was still slow. He had seen her before, only she had been wearing something different. Not jeans and a shirt, but a pretty dress. Pretty dress. Pretty name. He said, "Petal!" and she smiled beautifully; dark, happy eyes gleaming. She said, "So you've woke up at last. Thought you never would—got us quite worried."

There was a fat lady behind her with a round, rosy face. *Poll*, he thought, with relief. It was coming back now. She had rescued him from those horrible boys, brought him home with her. There was something else, too, something not so good, that he didn't seem to want to remember. But she had been kind, looking after him, letting him sleep here, waiting until he woke up before sending him home to his mother and father. . . .

Poll said, "Got a thick head, I should think, poor little cocker. Get something inside him, Petal. I can't stop, late already."

She went out of the front door and banged it behind her. Alex came slowly downstairs. "Where's she going?"

"Cleaning job, six to nine in the City. That's where she picked you up, isn't it?"

She went down the passage. Alex followed her into the kitchen where the boy with the HERE COMES TROUBLE T-shirt and the big man called Samson were sitting with their feet on the table. The kitchen was small and very untidy: dirty dishes and pans everywhere. "What a mess," Petal said. "Move your ugly great feet. The boy wants his breakfast."

Samson grinned. "You heard the lady, Jake. Move your plates of meat. Might upset our visitor's stomach."

Jake didn't move but Samson stood up, yawning and stretching, displaying a pelt of dark hair between his shirt and the top of his jeans. Then he pulled out a chair and pretended to dust it. "Sit yourself down," he said. "What do you fancy?"

Alex said, "I'm sorry. It's a bit late for breakfast."

"Not in this house. Liberty Hall. What'll it be? Smoked salmon? Caviar?"

"Eggs," Petal said. "Or there's a bit of that chicken Poll cooked for supper."

Alex remembered where the chicken had come from. Guilt made him queasy. He said, "I'm sorry. I'm not very hungry."

"He's sorry. He's not very hungry," Jake repeated. He swung his feet off the table and laughed in a sneering way, as if Alex had said something stupid.

"Hair of the dog, then," Samson said. "Got any tomato juice, pet? I'll fix 'im a Bloody Mary."

"Don't you dare," Petal said. "That was *wicked* last night. I thought you'd put water with it. Leave him be, Samson."

Samson shrugged his vast shoulders. "Okay, if you say so, lady. Just trying to help. Not often we entertain famous people. I'm out of the habit."

"Cut it out, Samson," Jake said.

Petal and Samson looked at each other. Jake watched them both. He had very pale eyes, very bright, as if lit from within. Petal said, in a subdued voice, "Leave him alone, both of you. I'll take care of him."

"Mind you do," Jake said. He left the kitchen, HERE GOES TROUBLE on his narrow back.

Before he followed him, Samson hugged Petal and kissed the top of her head. He winked at Alex. "Bit of all right, ain't she, kiddo?"

After he had gone, Petal didn't speak for a minute. She poured a glass of milk and cut a slice of bread. She cleared a space at the table and put the milk and the bread and a packet of butter in front of Alex. She sat opposite, watching him while he drank. Then she said, "There was a picture of you on the telly at lunchtime."

Alex swallowed a mouthful of milk the wrong way and choked. When he had finished spluttering, Petal said, "Run away from home, did you? What for? Did your Dad bash you up?"

"Course not," Alex said, shocked. "My Dad wouldn't hit me."

Petal laughed. "Okay! I just asked 'cos that's why I cleared off in the end. My Dad never could keep his fists to himself and he got so mad at me on account of the baby, I was scared he might hurt it." She saw Alex look at her stomach and patted it fondly. "You didn't think this was *me*, did you?"

"You can't tell with that floppy shirt," Alex said. "What did they say about me on the telly?"

"Just that you were missing, and showing your picture, and giving a number to ring. But Jake got the evening paper and that had a lot more. About your being adopted and inheriting money. Poll said . . ." She stopped. "Oh, never mind. You ought to eat something."

"I'm not hungry, I told you. What did Poll say?"

Petal said, rather fast, "Poll's been good to me. I got a job in a cafe but it was only temporary like, and I didn't have nowhere to sleep. Then Samson came in for a coffee and we got friendly and he brought me back here. The thing about Poll is, she doesn't ask questions."

She was frowning, her lovely eyes serious. She said, speaking more slowly and thoughtfully, "Samson's all right; he's a bit of a hulk, but he wouldn't hurt anyone. Nor would Bill. He's the punk. It's Jake you need to watch out for. He's young but he's mean."

"Watch out for what?"

Petal glanced at the closed kitchen door. She lowered her voice. "Jake can turn nasty. He pulled a knife on Bill yesterday, only a bit of an argument, but if Samson hadn't come in he'd have cut him. That's why I daren't risk anything, see? I've got to think of the baby."

She looked at Alex, still serious-eyed; then smiled and patted his hand. "Don't you worry," she said. "He won't touch you. Poll wouldn't stand for that and Jake knows which side his bread's buttered. But be a good boy and don't cheek him or anything."

Alex had almost stopped listening. All he could think of, quite suddenly, was how badly he wanted to be back at home. He could hardly remember why he had left. Only twenty-four hours, but it seemed like years, as if the Alex who had packed his bags yesterday had been someone else—another and much younger boy. Since then he had stolen meat from a supermarket, got drunk on brandy, slept in his clothes. He longed to be safe at home where such things couldn't happen. He thought—for the first time—*Mum must be worried.* He said, "Thank you for the milk, Petal. And please say thank you to Poll. But I think I ought to go home now. May I borrow your telephone?"

She was staring at him. He thought that perhaps they were too poor for a telephone. He said, "I don't know if I've got enough money for my fare. It was quite a long way, last night in the train."

She was still staring. He said, "My Post Office book got stolen last night, that's the trouble. I thought, if I rang, my mother would come to fetch me." His voice began to shake, he couldn't stop it. "I wish Mum would come," he said. "I wish she'd come soon. . . ."

He was afraid he was going to cry. He got off the chair and turned his face away. "Excuse me, I think I want to go to the lavatory."

Petal said, "You can't."

"But I *need* to go."

"No, love, I didn't mean that. Don't you understand? Poll said, *don't let him go.*"

It was his turn to stare. She said, with a sigh, "Don't look like that, treasure. No one's going to hurt you. It's just, Poll makes the rules; it's her house."

"But I don't want to stay. She can't make me."

His voice had risen to a shout. She said, "Ssh . . ." and looked at the door. "Oh, come on," she said. "It's not so bad here. What's your hurry? We'll play a game if you like."

"I don't want to play a game. I WANT TO GO HOME."

The door was flung open. Jake said, "Can't you keep the brat quiet?"

He came into the kitchen, thumbs stuck in the waist of his jeans, swaggering, grinning.

"He's upset," Petal said. "He wants to go home."

"I heard. What's he want to go home for? Ran away, didn't he?"

"I changed my mind," Alex said.

Jake put his grinning face close to Alex. He said, "Want me to change it back for you?"

Petal said, "Stop it, Jake. He's Poll's business, not yours."

Jake ignored her. He brushed Alex's cheek with his fingers. "Pretty boy, aren't you? I expect your Mum and Dad want their pretty boy back. So you'd better behave. Or I'll spoil your looks for you."

"Where's Samson?" Petal said.

"Out. Takin' the air. What d'you want him for?"

"Nothing. Just wondered."

Jake laughed. "Bill's not here either, in a manner of speaking. Wouldn't wake if you put a bomb under him."

Petal said, "Shall I make you a coffee, Jake?"

He looked at her, his light eyes expressionless, for what seemed a long time. There was nothing so frightening about Jake, Alex thought, those threats were just boasting. All the same, he held his breath until Jake began to smile slowly. He said, "Okay, then. Black for me, good and milky for my young brother here. We'll have it in the front room, just the two of us. Have a bit of a chat, no sweat, just sort things out nicely between us."

Chapter Thirteen

It was eight o'clock in the evening when Mr.
Fowles came. Laura had been helping her father
put Bob and Ellie to bed, and by the time they came
downstairs he was standing in the living room in his
raincoat, clutching his cap to his chest like a shield.
Laura's mother said, "George, you've met Mr. Fowles,
haven't you?" Her voice was a whisper with an edge
of fear to it.

Mr. Fowles said, "As I told your good lady, sir, I'd
have come before, only I was detained at the police
station."

He licked his harelip and grinned nervously. "I
think I satisfied them that I had nothing to do with
your boy's disappearance. I haven't come to intrude
on your grief, but to make an apology. I said a few
things to the lad that I shouldn't have said. I was fair
put out at the time, but that's no excuse."

"You frightened him," Laura said. "He was frightened."

"That's enough, Laura," her mother said. "Please

sit down, Mr. Fowles. We think we know now why Alex ran away. It wasn't your fault. It's kind of you to come."

"Just to show respect," he said. "Offer my condolences. A terrible thing to have a child missing." He sat, dangling his cap between his spread knees. "I want you to know that I don't bear him any malice. Nor you, either." His tone, which had been lugubrious, sharpened suddenly. "My quarrel is with the boy's grandmother. Though this isn't a time to go into that."

Laura's father said, "Would you like a drink, Mr. Fowles? Beer, or a glass of white wine? No trouble, my daughter will get it."

Trying to get rid of me, Laura thought. But to her satisfaction Mr. Fowles said, "No, thank you. I never touch liquor on principle. Nor coffee or tea. All harmful stimulants—an insult to the body. In any case, what I've come to say won't take long. Not a social visit, if you understand me."

He fell silent, twirling his cap, his eyes on the ground. At last he said, "I want you to know my position. I was riled to begin with. Wouldn't you be? If you'd looked after someone's affairs as long as I have, filled in her tax forms, seen to the house repairs, tried to take care of her, you'd have to be an angel not to resent it." He laughed suddenly. "Pardon the pun. Mind you, I can't say I liked my old Auntie. It was duty begrudged, and she didn't like me. Not educated enough to suit her! In fact, now I've gone off the boil a bit, I reckon she did it to spite me. If she hadn't left her money to the boy, she'd have cut me out some- how. I've no claim that would stand up in court my lawyer tells me, so I'll make no more trouble. You've got enough as it is." He shook his head solemnly.

"You're being generous, Mr. Fowles," Laura's fa- ther said. "Of course, if you find yourself out of pocket, I expect the estate will refund you."

"Hmm. Well. There is the little matter of the few small things I took from the house. I felt entitled, her only surviving relative, after all, but it seems the law may look at it differently."

Laura's mother said quickly, "I'm sure that will be all right, Mr. Fowles. Won't it, George? Though I suppose it isn't up to us, really. I mean, you said, *only surviving relative.* Do you mean that you think Mrs. Angel's daughter is dead?"

"She may be," Mr. Fowles said, speaking heavily, the lugubrious tone back in his voice again. "On the other hand, she may not."

Laura's mother and father looked at each other. Signals passed between them that Laura could not in- terpret. She stayed quiet and still, hardly breathing.

Mr. Fowles said, "Dorothy, her name was. Or is, as the case may be. Dorothy Angel. Unless she has changed it. Poor old Dorothy, tied hand and foot to her mother—not an easy life at her beck and call. No one else to carry the burden. *I can't stand it, Eric,* she said to me more than once. I said, why not clear off? But she'd shake her head. She was a good soul, not a match for that old devil, her mother. I was fair took aback, I can tell you, when she went in the end, walking out one morning with nothing except what she had on her back, and not a word from her after."

"Do you know where she went?" Laura's mother was leaning forward, her body tense, her face anxious.

Mr. Fowles sucked his brown teeth. "*Know* is pitching it strong. *Guess?* Well, maybe. There was a man she knew at the hospital. An Indian doctor. If her mother knew that, it wouldn't have pleased her. A colored bloke. *Any* bloke, come to that. Dottie was in her late thirties by then, the old cow must have reckoned she had her tied down, a slavey for life. Dottie would never have had the guts to stand up to her mother, so she took the easy road and bunked off. I hope that's what happened, I must say. I was fond of old Dottie. That's why I never said a word to her mother."

Laura's father cleared his throat. "Have you told your attorney?"

"He didn't ask. Only if I knew where she was now, and I don't. He wasn't keen to help me, so why should I bother? Besides, I thought I might have a word with you first. Since I'm out of the running, I can't see any reason to queer your boy's pitch. Eric Fowles isn't a dog in the manger! If Dottie turns up, that's one thing. If she doesn't—if she's married to her doctor and living in India or somewhere like that where she won't see the papers—then I thought, well, we might come to some sort of arrangement."

Laura heard her father make a strange sound, a

kind of snorting laugh that changed to a cough. He took out his handkerchief and blew his nose. "Sorry," he said. "Nothing doing."

"Okay, sir." Mr. Fowles sounded surprisingly cheerful. "Worth a try, though. No hard feelings!" He stood up, holding his cap to his chest again, grinning. "If you want to pass it on, the doctor's name was Chaudhuri. Dottie only mentioned him a couple of times, and I never saw him. But after she scarpered I rang up the hospital and they said that he'd left. I could have asked where he'd gone but I didn't. I wasn't that interested. If my Auntie had wanted to find out she could have done the same thing, talked to the hospital, asked about, but she didn't. Too blinking angry. That's why I guessed she had some idea where Dottie had gone. It's only the last couple of years she's moaned on about her lost daughter, her terrible sorrow. At the time, the names she called her aren't ones I'd care to repeat in front of a lady."

Laura's mother said, "Please, Mr. Fowles. There's something else. . . ." She closed her eyes, as if what she was thinking was so painful she could hardly bear it. When she opened them, they were dark and troubled. She said, "Tell me . . . you said you were fond of your cousin, so you might know . . . is it at all *possible* that she left home for another reason? Because she was pregnant and couldn't face telling her mother? That she had the baby, and then, because she couldn't look after it . . . ."

"I get you," Mr. Fowles said. "That's the story *your* mother was trying to feed my old auntie!"

She put her hands to her cheeks. Her face was one burning blush. "Not really. I expect she just said there was a resemblance between your cousin and Alex. I'm sure there was nothing more to it. My mother gets romantic notions sometimes, but she isn't a fool."

"More of a fool than my aunt! She may have been old, but she'd never have been taken in by that kind of rubbish. She had all her marbles! Even though I said different to start with, I knew it, really." He looked at Laura's mother, sucking his teeth, and then went on with unexpected gentleness. "She liked your boy, that was all. These last months, he was all she thought of. Oh, she wanted to spite me—taunted me with it—but leaving that aside, the feeling was there. She said, the last time I saw her, 'Such a dear child, Eric, so innocent. I'm afraid life will be hard on him.' As for Dottie, she was the last person to have a baby and dump it. Last thing in the world she'd have done. Dotty about babies was Dottie!"

He laughed. Laura's mother smiled weakly. She said, "Thank you, Mr. Fowles. I'm so sorry."

"Don't mention it." Mr. Fowles put his cap on and turned on his heel. He said, over his shoulder, as he left the room, "I shall pray for your boy."

Laura's father went with him. Her mother put her head in her hands. Tears leaked through her fingers. "Oh," she said, "I'd give anything . . . even if she was his mother . . . *whoever* she was, if she was alive and wanted to see him, I wouldn't mind. I could bear it, bear *anything* as long as he's safe, comes safe home, nothing else matters. . . ."

Laura watched her. For a second she thought—*She wouldn't cry like that if it was me that was missing. Only for Alex.* But then she knelt in front of her, took her hands and coaxed them away from her face. She said, "Don't cry, Mum. Please don't cry. You're making *me* cry. He'll come back."

She had a wonderful idea suddenly, exploding like a huge firework, brilliant sparks leaping and dancing. She said, dazzled and breathless, "Or we'll find him! *I'll* find him! I know a good way!"

Her mother said, "Oh, you darling!"

Laura sat back. She was pleased that her mother had called her *darling*, but she was embarrassed, too. In a minute her mother would ask her how she meant to find Alex, and she would have to tell her, and her mother would laugh. The idea wouldn't work if her mother laughed.

But although she did laugh, it wasn't at Laura. She said, laughing and crying together, "Laura darling, you've been such a comfort. I love you so much, you know that now, don't you?"

Chapter Fourteen

Dear Mum and Dad,

I hope you are well. I am quite well at the moment and hope to see you quite soon. I had my Post Office book stolen and my solar calculator. I am sorry I ran away. I want to come back. The people I am staying with are quite nice but I would rather be at home. Give my love to Laura and say that I hope she found my front door key and that I hope you will let her keep it because she didn't mean to be late home from Carla's party so it wasn't really fair to take hers away. Give my love to Bob and Ellie and Gran and tell Gran that I hope Major Bumpus is well. I miss everyone very much.

That was as far as he'd got. Looking over his shoulder, Jake said, "Only *quite* nice, are we?"

"Well, you're not very nice or you'd let me go home and not wait for Poll to come back."

Jake laughed and punched his back lightly. "Okay, shrimp, get on with the letter."

"There's nothing else to say, really. I mean, if it's a

kidnap letter, asking for ransom money, I'm not going to write about that."

"They'd pay up, wouldn't they?"

"It depends on how much you asked for, I suppose."

"How much do you think?"

"I don't know." He looked at Jake hopefully. "It's only a game, isn't it?"

"That's what you think."

"Poll didn't kidnap me. I asked if I could go home with her."

"Maybe she's changed her mind. You turned out to be a bit special. Have to wait and see, won't we?"

Alex yawned. It seemed that he had been sitting in this small stuffy room, lights on and curtains drawn although it was still daylight outside, for ever and ever. He thought that he ought to be scared and miserable and he had been a bit to begin with, but now he was too bored to be anything much. For a while they had watched a cricket game on the television and Petal had come in twice, bringing mugs of horrible coffee and egg sandwiches made with stale, white bread, stiff as cardboard. Otherwise, nothing had happened until Jake had started on the idea of writing the letter. There were no books in the room: nothing to read, nothing to do. Alex looked at his watch. He put it to his ear.

"Stopped, has it?" Jake said. He had thrown himself on the sofa, skinny legs dangling over the end, waggling one foot in time to the thump of the music coming down through the ceiling. Bill must have woken up, but he hadn't appeared. Samson hadn't come back. Alex wondered if Jake felt as bored as he did. He said, "No, it hasn't stopped. It's still only half past eight."

"What did you think?"

"About midnight. That's what it feels like. Don't you ever go out, Jake?"

"What's there to go out for?"

"Walking, or something."

"Walking! Catch me! 'Sides, I'm keeping an eye on you, ain't I? Working out how much you're worth. That's hard brain work. What d'you think? I expect your Mum and Dad would pay up sharp enough if we chopped off your ear and sent it along with that letter. Five thousand would be about right, I should think." He sniggered and looked slyly at Alex. "Or would you rather we made it a finger?"

"Don't be silly," Alex said.

"Silly, is it? You'd laugh on the other side of your face if I did it."

"You'd need a very sharp knife."

"What's this, then?" Jake took a long, slim knife out of his pocket. The blade sprang open.

Alex sighed. "If you came at me to cut off my ear, I'd throw you. A single arm shoulder throw. I learned how to do it last month in my judo class."

"Cool, ain't you?"

Jake was fingering his knife, pouting his lower lip, his bright, pale eyes narrowed. *Putting on his dangerous face,* Alex thought wearily. He said, "I'm too bored to be frightened."

Jake chuckled. "Okay. Let's do something, then." He stood up, holding the knife with the shining blade pointing at Alex. "Give you a fair chance. Get yourself ready."

"Put the knife down," Alex said. "I'm not a black belt, only green. That's just one up from the bottom."

He stood in the center of the room, waiting. Jake put the knife down on the arm of the sofa. "Don't you touch it," he warned. "If you do, tell you straight, you won't live to use it."

He darted at Alex. The next second he was on his back, on the floor. Alex held out his hand to pull him up. "It's quite easy," he said. "Shall I show you again?"

"No thanks. I believe you." Jake slumped on the sofa, rubbing his shoulder.

"I could teach you a bit if you like," Alex said. "Not that throw. You'd have to learn some of the basic things first."

"Kid's stuff," Jake said. "If I'd had the knife, you couldn't have done it. Not much use in a real fight."

"I've never been in a real fight. Not with knives." Alex thought he had better not boast. He said, "I expect I'd be too scared to do anything."

That seemed to please Jake. He said, "Glad you got a bit of sense. Kid like you could get in dead trouble. So don't get too cocky jus' because you caught me in a good mood. Don't try anything."

"No, Jake. Will Poll be home soon?"

"Never know, Saturdays. Sometimes she goes down the pub with her mates. She gets overtime money, weekends. It burns a hole in her pocket."

"She'll let me go home when she does come back, won't she?"

"Search me. You can't tell with Poll. She gets funny ideas. She don't like to be told what to do. And you put her in a bit of a spot—being in the news, like. So you better not ask too much, see? Just leave it to her to figure out the best way."

"Best way for what? How long will she make me stay here? What for? She's not really going to ask my parents for money, is she?"

"Thought I told you not to ask questions."

Jake was scowling ferociously. He threw himself on his back and glared at the ceiling. "Turn that row down!" he shouted. "D'you hear, Bill? If you don't, I'll come up and fix you."

A thud of feet shook the ceiling. The music stopped. Jake said, "Right. Bit of peace now."

Alex said, "I've got to ask something. I don't understand. It's not *fair*."

Jake was eyeing him thoughtfully. His eyes glinted. He said, "Poll's taken a fancy to you, that's the thing. Pretty boy, helps carry the groceries, doesn't look the sort to go thieving. Might turn out useful. Though it ain't only that." He chewed on his lower lip. "Bill was a pretty boy once."

Alex said, with horror, "You can't steal children

and make them go thieving! That's the sort of thing happens in *books*."

"Mebbe old Poll's read a book or two in her time. But I told you that wasn't the whole of it. Poll don't do anything, like, *deliberate*. Jus' goes along with what happens. People come an' go, sometimes she likes them to stay. And she wouldn't be stealing you from your Mum and Dad, would she? They adopted you— like stealing you from someone else, wasn't it?"

"That's not the same thing at all, I was *found*," Alex said. He was terrified suddenly. He didn't believe the things Jake was saying, but he knew now why Petal was scared of him. Jake was clever. He hadn't been able to frighten Alex with his dangerous flick knife, so he had thought of another way. He said desperately, "But she can't keep me here, keep me prisoner! That's against the law. They'll find out, the police will find out, and *she'll* go to prison!"

Jake was smiling. "The police aren't so smart! Hundreds of kids disappear every year. They don't find them, do they? What makes you think you're so special?"

"I'm not . . ." Alex stopped. There was no point in arguing. It was a sort of game Jake was playing but there were no rules except the ones that he made and he changed them as he went along. He was tormenting Alex because he was bored, making up lies about ransom notes and child stealers to frighten him. And that wasn't the worst thing. The worst thing was that no one in this house seemed to be sensible. If they were sensible people they would ring up his parents and let him go home. Even when Poll did come back, they might just sit around doing nothing except play silly games, keeping him here for ever and ever. . . .

He said, "If you don't let me go, I'll scream. I'll scream and scream . . ."

And, to his own amazement, he did. He opened his mouth and the sound seemed to come leaping out as if it had been blowing up like a great gust inside him—a shrill, whistling and wobbling scream, like a siren. He screamed and screamed and the scream turned into words. *"Let me go, let me go, LET ME GO . . ."*

His head was full of noise. A long way away, faint and distant, he could hear other sounds, voices shouting. He stood stiff and straight, eyes screwed tight shut, yelling louder and louder to drown the voices outside of him until his throat hurt, his mouth dried. Then someone was lifting him. He kicked, flailed his arms, but strong hands were holding him, shaking him, and at last his strength went, and he hung limply between them.

Chapter Fifteen

"There was this preacher," Laura said. "In a tent on the Fields at the time of the Easter fair. Alex and I went to the Meeting. They were all praying, but it wasn't like an ordinary church. They were waving their arms about and calling out names, asking the Lord to help them find missing people. I thought if we could find him, find the preacher, I mean . . ."

Her voice faltered. They were all looking at her so sadly: her mother and father, her grandmother, and Major Bumpus. Though the Major looked more thoughtful than sad, Laura decided, his bright blue eyes fixed intently upon her. Gran had seen Mr. Fowles leave the house and come to see what had happened, introducing the Major. "Monty is very experienced," she had explained, without saying what he was experienced *in*. Perhaps, Laura thought, she had wanted him for protection. Mum wouldn't pick a quarrel while the Major was there. Not that she seemed in the mood for quarreling just at the moment. She was sitting next to Gran on the sofa and holding Gran's hand.

She said, "Laura, darling, I don't think . . ." Her voice faltered too.

Major Bumpus said, "A trifle farfetched, maybe. But no point in leaving any stone unturned in this situation. Boy runs away, that's one thing. Boy *stays* away, that's another. Though whether . . ." He stopped abruptly. "Sorry," he said. "You don't want an old buffer like me shooting his mouth off. Amy asked me to come, and I'm willing, of course. Any help I can offer. But not interference. Last thing you want at this junction is interference from strangers."

"You're not a stranger, Monty," Laura's grandmother said. "You're one of . . ." She blushed a little. "That is, a friend of the family."

"Harrumph," Major Bumpus said. "Thank you, Amy."

"We're glad to have you here," Laura's father said. "The more help the better. If only we could think where he might have gone. We've asked all his friends at school, obviously. Other boys in his judo class. Neighbors. We're at our wits' end where to turn now."

"Perhaps Laura's right," her grandmother said. "Perhaps we should pray. Faith can move mountains."

"It may not find a little boy, though," Laura's mother said, with a return of her usual tartness. Then she looked at Major Bumpus and added politely, "But as you say, no stone left unturned." The phrase seemed to amuse her. She glanced at Laura's father and Laura saw a private smile pass between them.

Major Bumpus said, "I've a lot of time for prayer, though I'm not a religious man myself. But there are more things in heaven and earth. Come to that in a minute. Now. The boy wasn't taken from home, seduced away by some stranger, we've established that, haven't we? Whatever has happened since, he left on his own accord. Took his things with him. Upset. You ever wanted to run away, Laura?"

"Sometimes." She looked at her mother and father: a cold, threatening look, daring them to smile at each other.

"Right," Major Bumpus said. "No need to go into reasons. Always reasons in families. Where would you run to?"

"I don't know. I might go to Carla's house. She's my best friend. But that wouldn't be *serious*. I mean, it's the first place they'd look for me."

"Ah! So young Alex was serious, then, in your opinion?"

Gran said, "Monty, dear, do you think . . . I mean, how can she know? She's only a child."

"That's why I'm asking her, Amy. More likely to know certain things than the rest of us. Closer to the boy. But that isn't all. A young girl may have powers. Instincts, if you prefer the word. Sort of thing most of us lose as we get older. The spirit gets stiff, like the joints. Not in all cultures, of course. I've known quite old men in India . . ."

Gran said gently, "Is that relevant, Monty?"

"I think so. Give me time, dear. Don't mind a few questions, young Laura?"

She shook her head. The Major was watching her closely, as if what she might say was important. She felt pleased, if a little embarrassed. She said, "I think Alex was serious. He was really unhappy. Some of it was my fault. Some of it wasn't. He ran away because he thought he'd upset everyone—because he was being a nuisance."

"Would that make you run away?"

"No. Only if I was angry. To *make* them upset. If I'd been adopted, like Alex, and Mum and Dad had been foul to me, I might want to run away to find my real mother and father. But Alex is, I don't know, *different.*"

Major Bumpus nodded. "Right, then. You know that. The next bit is harder. Can you jump over that difference? Bridge the gap? Think how Alex would think, not how you'd think, in his place. Put yourself in his skin?"

She thought—I can do that sometimes with Ellie. She said, "I could try."

"Good girl. Tell me, now. What did you feel in that tent at the Meeting?"

"Sort of excited. It's hard to explain. A *fierce* kind of feeling."

"Prayer concentrates the mind," the Major said. "That's what I want you to do. Not pray, necessarily, unless you find that it helps. Think of Alex. All that you know about him. Fix your mind on him. Think of him on his own. Where he'd go, what he'd do. Any ideas come, even if they seem silly, don't fight them. Let them come, let them go—accept what they leave behind. Understand, do you?"

They were all looking at her. Dad cleared his throat. He was frowning, uncertain. Mum said, "Really, Major Bumpus, this is a bit mystical, isn't it?" She gave a little tight laugh. "Laura's not a clairvoyant."

"You don't know what I am," Laura said. She turned her back on her mother. She said, to Major Bumpus, "I can't do it here."

He nodded gravely, dismissing her. Lingering outside the room she heard him say, "Now. This feller, Fowles. Bit of a turn around, what? D'you trust him? How does it strike you, this tale about his cousin and the Indian doctor? Pinch of salt department, in my view. Makes you wonder if he's got someone up his sleeve—some woman he thinks might fool the lawyers. That's not our concern at the moment, though you may like to think about it. What we've got to consider is the boy's state of mind about Dorothy Angel. His grandmother had a fanciful notion. Sorry to embarrass you, Amy, but we need all the cards on the table in this situation. Did Alex cotton on? If he did, how did it affect him? Boys can be romantic about their mothers. Especially if there's a mystery."

Laura felt laughter gurgle inside her. She thought— Keeping them busy! Taking over. Taking over Gran would be a good thing. And making Mum and Dad think about Alex. She'd have to think, too. Did Major Bumpus really believe all that stuff? Half religious, half magic. Or was he just keeping *her* busy? Though she'd started it, hadn't she? So she'd better try. Even if it made her feel silly.

She went upstairs, into Alex's room. It was tidy and empty. She stood on the rug by the bed and closed her eyes to think better. Alex was somewhere. How could she find him by *thinking*? The Major had said, let ideas come, let them go. She heard Alex's voice in her mind. *You're not me.* That wasn't much help! She said—crossly, as if he were there in the room with her—"Trust you to be awkward."

She squeezed her eyes tighter, remembering something else suddenly. Alex's face when they left the Meeting had been shuttered and secret. What had he been feeling? He hadn't liked all that moaning and crying. He didn't believe you could find people that way. Or didn't want to believe it. Had he been afraid they might be able to find his real mother?

She said in a low voice, feeling foolish, "Listen, God, we're looking for Alex. Oh, that's silly. I mean, if You're there, You know that already. But if You don't mind, if You've got a bit of spare time at the moment, perhaps You could help us to find him. Help me concentrate. Give me a clue. Something like that."

That didn't sound right. She thought of the people in the tent, swaying and shouting. Perhaps you had to talk in that kind of church language, the words He was used to, speaking loudly as if He were deaf. She rocked a little, backward and forward, experimentally. She said, in a groaning singsong, "Dear Lord, help me to find my lost brother, Alex, and bring him home to comfort his family." That was more like it. "Oh, Lord, enter me with Thy spirit." She rocked her body more violently.

Nothing happened. She only felt giddy. She opened her eyes and sat down on the bed. Her mind felt quite blank. An empty balloon with nothing inside it. She shut her eyes again and doubled her hands into fists and pressed them against her closed lids. Lights flashed, white and red. She thought hard about Alex. He had very dark eyes and pale hair and a gap between his front teeth. He liked judo, and roller skating, and computer games. He didn't like football or cricket, though Dad said he had a good eye for a ball. He had got first prize on the shooting range at the Easter fair. He liked animals. At school he was best at nature study and math. He was eleven years old. He was small for a boy of eleven. Last year he had measured himself every morning, standing with his back to the door and a ruler pressed on his head, to see if he had grown in the night. Dad had told him to stop. He had said watched pots never boiled. Dad had been quite short until he was fourteen, when he had shot up like a bean. Of course that didn't mean Alex would grow like that, since he was adopted and his real parents might have been midgets, but he had believed Dad all the same. Alex always believed what you told him. And he had got a bit fatter, lately. He had once been so thin, with little thin legs! Froggie, Dad had called him, as he lifted him out of the bath—oh, years ago, now—leaving Laura in the water and sitting on the toilet seat with Alex wrapped in a warm towel on his lap, cuddling him. And Laura, watching, had remembered Dad holding her like that when she had been smaller—warm, rough towel under damp bottom—and known exactly how Alex was feeling, cuddled and close and safe on Dad's lap. *Inside Alex.* She pressed her fists tighter against her hot eyeballs and felt something coming. Froggie. Frogs. Alex and frogs. No, not frogs, *toads.* The feeling was very fierce now. *Alex with a toad in his hand.*

She opened her eyes. She said, hearing herself sound like her mother, "Oh, how ridiculous!" It really was crazy. The Major was crazy! She should never have been taken in! She had done what he said, concentrated, fixed her mind, and all that came in was a *toad*!

She laughed out loud. She had half a mind to march straight down and confront him. Tell him how stupid he was, tell him the dumb thing that had come into her head. Tell Mum and Dad to stop listening to him. All this time they were sitting about, listening and talking and doing this foolish thinking to please the old Major, something terrible might be happening to Alex. Something must have happened already, or he'd have come back by now. Unless he were too scared that they'd be angry.

No. He wouldn't be scared of that. But he might be

scared no one wanted him. Once you'd run away, it could be hard to come back for all sorts of reasons. It would be hard for her, anyway. Alex was different, not so stubborn and proud, but she couldn't be Alex. She couldn't think herself into him. She had tried and it hadn't worked. So what would *she* do? Ring up Carla and say where she was? Or wait somewhere sensible. Sit in a park where there were lots of people to see her and wonder why she looked so lonely and lost. Hang about near a police station. Wait until she was *found* . . .

The fierce feeling was back, squeezing her chest, almost stopping her breathing. Of course she knew where Alex would go! She wasn't guessing, she *knew*. She waited for her breath to come back, and then went downstairs to tell them.

Chapter Sixteen

"That's better," Samson's voice said. He thumped Alex down on a chair and tugged at his hair, forcing his head back. He said, "He'll listen now, Poll."

Alex opened his eyes. Poll's red, shiny face was so close he could smell her warm, oniony breath. She said, "Soft little mutt! What a carry on! *Let me go, let me go*, what d'you think we're goin' to do? Keep you here? D'you think I ain't got enough on my plate?"

"Jake," he moaned. "Jake said . . ."

"Just a bit 'o fun." Jake's sullen voice came from somewhere behind him. "Silly tyke can't take a joke, Poll. 'Sides, you told us . . ."

"I said, keep 'im here till I'd thought what to do. Not scare the kid witless. You clear out, Jake. Clear out the lot of you. I'm warning you now, I'm not cooking in that mucky kitchen, so if you fancy your dinner you'd better get started."

They had gone. Poll sat on the sofa, knees spread, gently massaging her stomach. She belched comfort-

ably and said, "Heard you right down the street. Anyone 'ud think you was being murdered."

He said, "Jake's got a knife."

"Jake's a bad lad. Only a lad, though. Someone's
got to give him a chance. That's why I got to be careful. Couldn't just let you run home, could I, lovey?
Not with half London out looking for you. I've got to
think of my boys, see? I can't have the police 'round
here, asking questions."

He wondered what Poll's "boys" had done. Perhaps
Jake had knifed someone and the police were trying
to find him. He longed to know, but it seemed rude to
ask. And, possibly, dangerous. Poll was a thief. Perhaps they all were. Perhaps there were a whole lot of
stolen things hidden here. Nothing in this room
looked particularly new or valuable except the huge
color telly, but there might be another room, a locked
room, full of treasures.

Poll was bending over, grunting as she pushed off
her slippers. Her bare feet looked painful: swollen,
pink toes and lumpy blue veins around her ankles. He
said, "My Gran's feet get sore sometimes. She soaks
them in a bath of salt water."

"D'you live with your Gran?"

"No. I live with my Mum and Dad and my brother
and sisters. Bob and Ellie and Laura. But our Gran's
house is opposite, on the other side of the Fields."
Thinking of the Fields, of the lights that would be
coming on in the houses at this time of the evening,
beaming out yellow and friendly, made his throat

[144]

ache. He said, "Please, Poll, if you let me go home, I won't say where I've been. I won't say about Jake, or Samson, or anyone. Even if they asked me, I couldn't. I mean, I don't know where I *am*. When we came last night, I was sleepy. I didn't even notice the name of the station."

But he would see it on the way home, of course. And he hadn't been sleepy in the supermarket! He saw with horror the fix he was in. How could Poll trust him to keep his mouth shut? If the police found out she'd taken him stealing, she might go to prison. He said, miserably, "I won't tell, I promise."

To his surprise, she started to laugh. Her body shook and rippled with laughter. "I thought you was just a poor little cocker, nowhere to go, needing a bed. Not likely the police will swallow that, is it? They'll want to know what old Poll's bin up to this time, and I can't say as I blame them. Kidnapping a young millionaire—my Lord, when I read it all in the papers you could've knocked me down with a feather."

He said, hope springing suddenly, "I expect there might be a reward. Jake made me start a letter, asking for ransom money. That was a game. But I expect if I told my Mum and my Dad you'd been kind to me . . ."

Her laughter broke out again, making her wheeze. "Bless you, lover boy," she said, when she was able to speak. "I don't want your money. All I want is to keep out of trouble. Enough of that in this sad old life without looking for more. And it ain't just the boys

I've got to watch out for. There's Petal. She's dead scared her Dad will find out where she is and lug her off home. She's only fifteen. Underage, see?"

He hardly heard her. Something she had said before was too loud in his mind. He said, shyly—wanting very much to know but feeling embarrassed about it—"I don't know how much money there is. What did it say in the paper?" He felt himself growing hot. He thought, Mum and Dad would be angry if they knew I was asking. But he asked, all the same, "I'm not really a millionaire, am I, Poll?"

"Gettin' on that way. About eight hundred thousand, it said." She shrugged her shoulders as if this was nothing much. Or too much, perhaps; more than she could take seriously. She looked at him and chuckled. "It ain't like being Paul Getty, exactly."

"It seems an awful lot to me," he said, quite severely, wondering how someone so poor that she had to steal food for supper could be quite so casual about such a vast fortune.

"Depends how you look at it, laddie. If it was all spending money, that's one thing. But Jake says he expects the lawyers will get their greedy paws on a good chunk of it. And if the old girl's daughter turns up, you'll have to split it between you. Time they've taken off tax, you'll have 'bout enough to buy a house, that's what Jake reckons. Think of money in terms of houses, is what Jake always says, an' you cut it down to size. Mind you, a roof over your head ain't a bad start in life, I'd not have said no, I c'n tell you."

She grinned at him and he grinned back. He felt suddenly easier. She was so straight and friendly. Jake had said, *Poll doesn't ask questions.* But he felt he could ask her anything. He said, "Do you think that they'll find her? Mrs. Angel's daughter?" He thought of the dark eyes watching him from the picture. He looked at Poll. He said, "My sister Laura said she might be my real mother. That's why Mrs. Angel left me the money. Do you think she could be?"

"Can't tell you that, dearie, can I? Though if she was, then it's my guess she ain't around any longer. Leavin' you where she did, by the river."

"I don't understand."

"Don't you, lovey? Well, mebbe it ain't my business to tell you. Though I know what it's like . . ." She was quiet for a little, watching him with a worried look. Then she said, "I was a foundling, like you. Only I wasn't so lucky. Grew up in an orphanage. People used to visit sometimes, looking for a kiddie to take home with them to adopt into their family. When that happened, I always hoped *this time they'll pick me.* No one ever did. Can't blame them, can you? I always was a great, ugly, fat lump. You'd have been all right, though, with your pretty face and nice ways. Not surprising your Mum and Dad took a shine to you."

He said, "Laura says my real mother must worry about me, wondering if I'm all right and if I think about her. I used not to, but I've started now."

"Well, that's natural, ain't it? My Mum left me on

the church steps. I often think of her, leavin' me there when it could have bin anywhere. It was a sin in those days, a kid with no father, it's as if she was asking God to forgive her. Tellin' me to be Christian, like. Your Mum left you by the river. I reckon she did that for a reason."

Alex said, "Dad says she couldn't look after me." He felt a sudden, sad anger. "If I had a baby, I mean I know I can't because I'm not a girl, but if I was a girl and I did, *I'd* look after it."

Poll said, "Expect she did her best, that's how you got to think of it. She carried you as long as she could, set you down when her arms couldn't hold you no longer. Tired of life. Not everyone's strong enough. So she left you where she knew someone 'ud find you and know where she'd gone, what she'd done. D'you understand now?"

He didn't answer. He didn't want to think about it. He felt too numb and afraid.

Poll said, "Don't look so sad, cocker. Let the poor soul rest in peace. She wouldn't want you to fret. You love your Mum and Dad, don't you?"

He nodded, speechless. She said, "Then you're a lucky lad. Good parents, nice home, I daresay. Ought to be ashamed of yourself, runnin' off like that. They'll be out of their minds with the worry. Didn't think of that, did you?"

He found his voice. "That's not fair. I mean, I know I didn't think to begin with, but it isn't fair now. It was you who told the others I couldn't go home. You're the one stopping me."

[148]

He wondered if he should start screaming again. Poll said she had heard him right down the street. If he screamed the neighbors might hear this time, call the police . . .

But Poll was laughing again. Wheezing and laughing. "Course you're going home. Just a matter of bein' careful. Jake will think of a way, he's got brains. Long as you do what you're told and no nonsense. You wouldn't want to make trouble for poor old Poll, would you? Come 'ere a minute."

He got off his chair and went to her. She took his hands and held him between her knees, looking up at him. He could smell the onions on her breath, and her sweat. She was an ugly old woman and not very clean. But she was a kind person. He said, "I'm sorry you had to stay in the orphanage. If I'd been a grown-up, I would have chosen you."

She cackled at that, but in a pleased, friendly way—laughing with him, not at him. She said, "Get along, you soft ha'porth, if you go on like that I'll be startin' to think I don't want to lose you."

It was lovely riding pillion on Samson's big bike. Alex had been alarmed to begin with, when Jake first tied the scarf around his eyes, but in a way being blind made it much more exciting—all sound and motion, the roar of the engine, the smooth tilt and swoop as the bike rounded corners. Pressed close to Samson's leather jacketed back, arms clinging around him, he felt both safe and exhilarated—part of the beautiful, powerful machine, moving with it. Twenty times, *fifty* times better than skating! *Like being a huge bird,* he thought, *free and graceful.*

He could have gone on forever, flying blind through the warm night. When the bike stopped and Samson lifted him off the pillion he staggered, losing his balance. Samson caught his arm and unfastened the scarf. He said, "Okay, kiddo. On your own now. Know where you are? Where old Poll picked you up, just about."

They were in a quiet, narrow street. Lamps threw yellow puddles of light. Dark beyond them. A mournful hoot from the river. Alex said, "Near the Embankment."

"Right," Samson said. "Back where you started from an' no hassle. Smart lad, our Jake."

"He didn't have to blindfold me," Alex said. "I wouldn't have told anyone where I'd been."

"Better safe than sorry," Samson said. He got back on the bike, and grinned down at Alex. He said, "Nice knowing you, kiddo."

Suddenly, Alex didn't want him to go. He said, "Thank you for the ride. It was *fabulous,* Samson. I wish I had a motorbike . . ."

But Samson was revving up too loudly to hear. He shouted, "Straight home now. No more messing about."

The noise of the engine echoed back from the dark walls on either side. After that, silence. Sunday night, the City was empty of people, dark and mysterious. Like a city of the dead, Alex thought, a bit fearfully.

He hurried away from it, down to the river—to the welcoming lights strung along the Embankment, and, a short walk away, an Underground station. The last bus had probably gone, but there might be a train. At home they would be in bed by now. He would have to ring the bell, wake them up. Mum and Dad wouldn't mind, but he hoped that Bob and Ellie wouldn't be scared at someone coming to the door late at night. He worried about that, a little, but it wasn't until he got to the station and felt in his pocket that real anxiety seized him. He had no money. Not enough for his fare, anyway. Three two-pence pieces and one half-penny. That was enough for the telephone. But there was only one kiosk inside the station. And the sign on the door said OUT OF ORDER.

Several people were going through the barrier to the trains. Most of them seemed in a hurry, purposeful, looking straight ahead. There was one lady with a kind face he thought he could ask, but he hesitated too long. Before he could reach her, she had followed the others. Now there was only a man left, putting coins into the ticket machines. Alex stood beside him. He said, "Please, sir . . ." The man turned and looked at him. One side of his face was quite ordinary, the other was shockingly and hideously scarred, with what looked like a bunch of purple grapes hanging from the shrunken socket where his eye should have been. Alex stammered, "I'm s-sorry . . ." And ran.

Out of the station he was ashamed almost at once. It must be dreadful to look so frighteningly ugly that people run away from you. But he was afraid to go back—afraid even to look back over his shoulder, in case he should see the man staring after him.

He walked on, whistling softly under his breath. He could walk home. It was only about six miles, it wouldn't take much more than an hour and a half. But the way home lay through the deserted, dark City. And he was tired. His legs were tired, and his mind. Once he got home there would be so many questions.

He hadn't meant to visit the scene of his Finding, but when he came to Cleopatra's Needle with the two bronze Sphinxes either side, it seemed a natural and comforting place to be. He climbed the steps and sat between the arms of the left-hand Sphinx, knees drawn up to his chest, head resting against the cold stone, watching a long barge gliding past. Ripples widened slowly behind it, flashing silver where the light caught them, rocking the water against the wet walls below him.

It was very peaceful. The bridges arched beads of light across the dark water and the river flowed under them, thick and wrinkled and slow. Poll had said that his mother had been tired of life. She had said, let her rest in peace. *Peace* was a sweet word. His mother had laid him down here, in the arms of the Sphinx, and gone into the quiet, peaceful river, like a mermaid going home to the sea. He thought about that with a kind of sad wonder, seeing her for a moment quite clearly, young and dark-eyed like the girl in the photograph. Then she seemed to fade in his mind and other thoughts came.

He wished he could have a motorbike, a big one like Samson's. Perhaps Dad would let him buy one when he was older. Mum wouldn't like it. She would be frightened, but Dad might persuade her. He would be rich enough to afford it. Rich enough to buy a house, Poll had said. He would buy a big house by the sea and find people to live in it, go out to look for them and take them home with him—the lost children, the ugly ones, all the sad, lonely people. Laura could live with him too, and help him look after them, and make them happy again. And perhaps, when Mum and Dad were quite old, they would come too, and live in a big bright sunny room, facing the sea. . . .

He was yawning. His eyes were closing. His thoughts seemed to be floating away from him like the pieces of driftwood floating past on the river. Big Ben struck the hour, twelve solemn strokes booming downriver on a cool wind that stirred his hair gently, but he didn't hear them. He didn't hear the car stop. He didn't even hear Laura's excited laughter.

This time he was fast asleep when they found him.